BATTLE
EARTH VI

NICK S. THOMAS

First published in the United Kingdom
by Swordworks Books.

ISBN 978-1-909149-12-0

Typeset by Swordworks Books
Printed and bound in the UK & US
A catalogue record of this book is available
from the British Library

Cover design by Swordworks Books
www.swordworks.co.uk

BATTLE EARTH VI

NICK S. THOMAS

PROLOGUE

From the first entry in the journal of Colonel Mitch Taylor, 5th September 2138

Close to two years ago we fled the enemy system of Tau Ceti and left friends behind. We fully expected, and prepared, to continue the fight in our own territory. But the enemy never came. For a year the planet and outlying colonies continued under wartime conditions to ensure we could be at our very best. Every day that has gone by there has not been a human alive who did not expect and fear the return of the Krycenaeans.

The first war ravaged Earth and we barely held on. Through the quick advancements in technology that the alien technology provided, and the stubborn nature of all who fought to defend our lands, somehow we made it. The second war regained what we had lost, but was a bitter reminder of how powerful the enemy truly is.

Now civilians are beginning to doubt if we will ever see them again. Did we beat them? I hear people ask every few days. Did we show them this was a battle they could not afford to fight? I shrug my shoulders and mumble in response, all the time knowing in my heart the answer - No.

Many have tried to move on, and others say to enjoy every day we have in peace. Si vis pacem, para bellum - If you wish for peace, prepare for war.

CHAPTER ONE

Captain Ryan stepped out onto the bridge to begin his last week of the Deveron's posting to the Gateway. It was a duty no one in the Navy wanted, but it had to be done. Since the retreat from Tau Ceti the combined fleets of Earth had kept a permanent deployment at the strategically vital point.

But too much time had passed now with seemingly no response from the enemy to the invasion into their own lands. Support on Earth was once more waning through the short sightedness and hope that it was all over. Ryan woke each day knowing that it could be his last. The strength of the deployment had decreased substantially in the last month to just a dozen vessels.

As was typical, the Deveron was the smallest of all the fleet, but her crew were no less proud. He ran his hand along the rails. They were thick acrylic and room temperature, smooth to the touch, and reassuringly solid. He didn't know why he did that, but his connection with the ship made the Deveron feel like family.

Still going strong, he thought to himself. She had indeed been to hell and back.

"Anything to report?"

"No, Sir, no activity, as usual."

Despite having command since the death of Captain Reyes, he still felt awkward having taken his place. The crew loved Reyes, and in spite ofRyan being one of them for many years; they were big shoes to fill.

"Captain, I have an incoming private message for you."

"I'll take it in my quarters," he replied.

He hoped it was his wife and already knew it would be. He rushed off to see her face. He sat down quickly and accepted the message. He received such communicates every few days, but they could never have a live discussion. Frequently, their responses to each other would come long after they were relevant. It was frustrating, but that only made each message that bit more exciting. It was the only excitement in his life anymore. A posting to the Space Gateway was both deadly boring and immensely scary.

The screen came to life, and as always, she did not waste a second with getting into a cheery greeting. She flicked through their daughter's schoolwork with a smile. He could see the light of day seeping in from the window where she sat. It had been a beautiful sunny day when she had recorded the message. He turned away for just a second to see the blackness from his small loophole. He grunted at the comparison as he thought of where he could be and what he could be doing.

Ryan turned back and opened his mouth as if to respond to her there and then before the reality struck him. For a moment, when he looked away and heard her voice beside him, he could imagine she was there in the room. He leaned forward and merely gazed at her lips moving without really listening to what she was saying. To his surprise the audio suddenly cut off when she was mid sentence, and the screen faded away.

The Captain was about to hurl abuse at the console when an emergency warning light throbbed, and he realised something serious was happening. He hit the acceptance button. Lieutenant Wayans was projected before him.

"What is it?" he asked abruptly.

The precious little time he got to enjoy new messages from his family were the one thing in his life he could not tolerate having interrupted. But all of that anger vanished now, realising a serious matter lay ahead.

"Sir, we've got activity at the Gateway."

His heart sunk, and he stopped breathing for a moment. It was the last news in the world he would ever wish to receive. He finally caught a breath and came back to life.

"I'll be right out."

He stood up but was a little shaky. He'd seen enough

action against the Krycenaeans to wish he could never see another again; the very thought of their return struck fear into all humans. He shook the stiffness out of his body and regained his composure. He knew he could not afford to be off his game now. There had been no evidence of an enemy presence, but he already knew it would be them.

Ryan strolled out onto the bridge to find it almost silent. The crew stood or sat at their stations not knowing what to do. There was nothing to do yet. A few lights flickered on the Gateway. Ryan had seen this before. Something was coming through, and there was nothing they could do to stop it.

"I've got an incoming feed from the Collingwood, Sir," stated Lovett.

The ensign was young and the Deveron was her first posting, but she had so far proven her worth. But all Ryan could think was of the Collingwood, the largest vessel in the fleet. It was a cruiser that had been built during the last war and whilst powerful, it was a world apart from the two carriers that led the assault into Tau Ceti.

"Put it on screen," he replied.

Commodore Clark appeared and despite his quick address of the fleet, they could all see the terror in his eyes.

"You must all have noticed by now that the Gateway has become active. We must assume that something is coming through and that whatever that may be, they mean to do us harm. We were stationed here to guard the colonies of the Solar System against any such threat."

He took a deep breath and was clearly in shock that it was happening on his watch.

"I am sorry that it has fallen on all of you to bear this responsibility, but we must hold the Gateway at all costs."

All Ryan could think was that they didn't have enough ships. Not enough marines, not enough guns. They could repulse a reconnaissance or expeditionary force at the very most. Any serious invasion of the System would run right through them."

"We have been through these drills a hundred times. Prepare to defend yourselves, and God be with us all. Good luck."

The transmission ended and the bridge crew remained motionless and silent. Ryan wanted nothing more than to fire up the engines and make a run for Earth where the defence grid was operational and the main fleets were stationed. He knew everyone around him felt the same way, but he could not act upon it. He opened up a ship wide comms channel.

"This is the Captain speaking. We have incoming through the Gateway. All hands on deck! All weapons prepare to fire. Repair crews at the ready and blast doors sealed. We've got a fight on our hands. All marines prepare for boarding defence. You all know the drills, get to it."

Ryan knew the twenty-six marines on board would

be of minimal use should they get hit hard. Lieutenant Samson was a fine marine and a capable leader, but they needed more than just skills, they needed numbers. He turned to Wayans.

"Break open the weapons and armour. I want every crew member armed and ready to fight."

Several of the bridge crew overheard the order, and it was horrifying for them all. They had all served in the last war, but none had ever had to come face to face with the alien soldiers they had heard such harrowing stories of. They still remained motionless, and Wayans was startled by the orders.

"Get on it, Lieutenant."

The second-in-command coughed and finally responded in a growly voice from his dry throat.

"Aye, aye, Sir."

Samson arrived on the bridge just twenty seconds later. It was clear he had sprinted for the bridge the moment the Captain's orders were issued. He stopped for a moment as he caught sight of the viewing screen and the Gateway beginning to spin. The Marine officer had never seen it in operation before. He had spent his war fighting on the east coast of the US. Rarely had he had cause or desire to leave the States, and yet now here he was on the borders of the Solar System.

"It's really happening?" he whispered to the Captain.

Ryan nodded grimly in response.

"It's fair to say whatever is coming through that Gateway is not going to be friendly."

"I never thought I'd see them again. Didn't we mess 'em up enough the first time?"

"They gave as good as they got."

"If they come through in such numbers, we can't stand, so what's the plan?"

Ryan shrugged his shoulders.

"What is the plan, Captain? There must be some contingency."

Ryan shook his head.

"There is no plan beyond holding this area, no matter the cost."

Samson stepped even closer to be sure nobody could hear his faint words.

"The cost may well be every ship, sailor, and marine in this fleet if what comes through the Gateway is what we have always feared."

Ryan nodded in agreement.

There's no denying it. Fear is running rampant amongst the human fleet. Have we already lost the battle before it has even begun?

Ryan could not help but feel it, but he knew if he showed as such to the crew that it would be a self-fulfilling prophecy and would be the end of them all.

"Sir, just promise me you won't throw all our lives away needlessly," Samson asked of him.

It was the catalyst Ryan needed. His head snapped

around to make eye contact with Samson, and he took a quick step back to address him as the Captain.

"I have no intention of doing so, Lieutenant. Let's not forget who and what we are. We are the victors of the greatest war in human history. We have fought off everything that has been thrown at us. Man your post. If we get boarded, you'll more than have your hands full."

Never having been in space, Samson had not witnessed the brutal boarding actions of the alien forces. Though he had been thoroughly informed and trained in the response to such actions, of which many other marines had become familiar with. Samson was well aware that the Deveron once carried Colonel Taylor and his Inter-Allied force. It was a lot to live up to.

"I'll have five marines posted to the bridge for the duration," he replied.

Ryan acknowledged with gratitude. The marines had substantially more armour and firepower than was being issued to the crew. Their compact Reitech carbines were a big step up from anything pre-war, but the full battle rifle was still a far more potent weapon.

The Marine officer rushed off to organise himself. None of them had yet seen any enemy, but they could all feel their presence was imminent.

Why on Earth does it have to be now? Ryan asked himself.

He had always expected to be followed through the Gateway when they made their retreat from the fateful mission to Tau Ceti. He had prayed they had reached a stalemate, but clearly that was too much to hope for.

"Monitor our comms channels. I want to know if the jammer shielding is working."

Going dark everytime they engaged the enemy had cost a lot of lives. Reiter and the other military scientists believed they had devised a solution, but as yet, it was untested in combat. Their defences were as prepared as they could be. Now they could do nothing but wait and watch.

Lights flashed around the Gateway as it began to spin faster and faster. The swirling spiral of light erupted at its core, and the Gateway was finally open. For a few seconds nothing happened, and they wondered if there was anything coming through at all. It was too much to hope for.

The hulking bow of a huge enemy warship pierced the light. The intimidating prow quickly expanded out from the Gateway, revealing the superstructure. It was familiar to them all as an enemy heavy warship. Ryan felt his heart almost stop. His mouth was dry and a bitter taste was in his mouth. His head began to pulsate like a horrible migraine attack. A few drops of sweat dropped down from his scalp. One dropped into his right eye and the other his mouth. The salt only made the bitter taste in his mouth worse, and his eye felt the sting.

It was an unavoidable reaction to seeing the fearsome

enemy once again after having hoped and believed he'd never have to do so again. He wiped his brow with the sleeve of his uniform. The previously spotless grey tunic was now smeared with the sweat stain, but it was the least of his problems. He could not let the rest of the crew see the fear within him. Not only that, if he wanted to survive, he needed to have his wits about him.

Seconds later, other enemy vessels began to break through into the Solar System. They were just a few hundred metres from the Gateway when they hit the wall of mines that had been laid as a defensive measure for this very circumstance. They could not destroy the Gateway, but neither did they believe they would ever want to use it again. The minefield blocked off the entire entrance to all but a hidden path for small research vessels to get through.

The intimidating enemy vessel triggered a dozen mines that tore massive holes in its hull. Finally as it hit the fifteenth mine, the engines lost power, and it was crippled. Still with forward momentum, it continued to be pummelled by the wall of mines until it was nothing more than a floating hulk. The Captain wondered for a moment if they had hostile intentions. They had come through the Gateway and hit them first before anyone could know their purpose.

Years of warfare had taught all of humanity that the sight of Krycenaeans meant you were in grave danger, and that immediate violent action against such was your duty.

And yet Ryan's time amongst the two aliens in Taylor's unit had made him wonder otherwise.

None of it matters anymore. It's too much to hope they came in peace, anyway.

Ryan's crew gave out a cheer at the defeat of the first enemy ship, but it was a short-lived celebration. Even while the hulking enemy vessel continued to ignite further mines, the next wave was opening fire. A signal came up on screen from the Collingwood. It was a surprise to them all to see their comms were still working in the presence of the enemy, but they did not have time to celebrate.

"You are clear to fire in your own time. Give those alien bastards hell!" yelled the Commodore.

Ryan turned to his crew.

"You heard him, fire!"

The bridge crew of the Deveron were still stunned by the re-emergence of the enemy. Many were fresh recruits who'd replaced their fallen comrades after the Tau Ceti expedition. Vast light pulsed through space as the Collingwood bombarded the incoming ships.

The alien fleet could only come through the Gateway a few at a time, but there seemed no shortage of them. The first five were obliterated in the opening two minutes of the battle, but they were still gaining ground. A pulse smashed into the bow of the Deveron, shaking the crew violently. Damage reports were coming in quickly, but their guns were still firing.

Ryan could do nothing now but watch and hope that their firepower could stop the enemy in their tracks. There were no tactics here. It was a numbers game. He turned to see several crew dispensing armour and weapons to those on the bridge. He stepped up and grasped a rifle from one of them and slung it over him.

They were all feeling terrifyingly vulnerable to the enemy assault, and noone would want to come face to face with one of the alien soldiers without a weapon to hand. Ryan wished he'd had been issued an Assegai, which he had heard used to such effect, but they were not issue equipment to Navy crews. He turned back to the viewing screen to see the fire increasing in intensity.

Despite the immense amount of fire being lashed on the incoming fleet, it was not enough to bring them to a halt. Floating wrecks tumbled past the human fleet as many more took their place. A massive light burst impacted off to their one side as a barrage of fire smashed one of the human cruisers. Ryan could see lights going out as the stricken ship lost power. He could only hope some of the crew could get to the escape shuttles as there was nothing to be done for them.

"How are they still coming at us?" asked Wayans.

Ryan shook his head. He had no answer. He had seen the ferocity with which the enemy fought before, but he had also seen them broken and flee. Now they seemed to exhibit an unbreakable will to succeed, no matter the cost.

They were back and tougher than ever.

"We invaded their homelands. Remember how hard we fought back when they did it to us?" the Captain responded.

"Hardly the same thing, Sir. They started this war."

"I'm not sure it matters anymore the reasons why or who did what," he muttered.

Ryan fell silent once again. Most of the bridge crew could now do little but watch the carnage unfold before them.

"Sir! We have incoming assault craft!" yelled Wayans.

"Divert all fire to them! We can't let them get through!"

The Deveron's guns roared, and one of the craft was cut in half from the salvo. Fighters from the Collingwood approached in formation to try and stop them, but even as the first few craft were immobilised or destroyed, more pushed forward. A dozen of the assault craft burst through some of the wreckage, heading directly for the Collingwood. The fighters quickly came around, but they had little time to stop them.

Half of the enemy craft were blown apart, but the others smashed into the hull of their flagship.

"God save us," whispered Ryan.

He turned his attention back to the viewing screen and saw a salvo of enemy fire heading their way. Just a second later, the Deveron was rocked violently by multiple impacts, and the Captain was thrown off his feet. His head smashed into the Captain's chair. Despite being saved from death by his helmet, he instantly blacked out.

Ryan regained consciousness to see sparks and smoke emanating from the console at the front of the bridge. Crews were fighting to put out the flames. He could tell he had been out for just a minute or two, but it was still disorientating. His head throbbed so much it felt as if it were going to burst out of the helmet. Two of the crew were seriously hurt and were being attended to.

A hand slapped down on his shoulder and wrenched him around. His neck was limp, and his head flopped over before recovering. Wayans was kneeling over him and asking something, but his hearing was still dulled. Within just a few seconds it recovered, but Wayans had already resulted to shouting louder after realising he couldn't understand.

"Are you okay, Sir?"

The ear splitting shout hurt his ears further, making his eyes wince. The coarse and acrid electrical burning smell filled his nostrils, and for a moment, he wished to be dead and have it all over with. He nodded in response to Wayans' question. He reached forward and hauled him back onto his feet.

"Are you with us, Sir?" he asked.

"Yeah, yeah, I'm still here," he finally replied.

The ship was rocked again by a smaller impact that Ryan barely weathered. His knees wobbled, and he was feeling sick from the disorientation.

"Somebody give me an update!"

Wayans scrambled from one of the wounded crew to his console. Their viewing screen was down, and the Lieutenant was doing his utmost to get it back up and running. As he tapped away on the controls, he started to convey the info he had.

"The Manchester is destroyed. Damage is being reported throughout the fleet, and the Collingwood is fighting at multiple breaches in their hull, Sir."

"Are we holding?"

"At present, Sir, yes, but there seems to be no end to the enemy fleet coming through the Gateway."

Lights flickered as the display monitor came back online. Ryan gasped at the sight. The lights and glow of the revolving Gateway were barely visible anymore over the mass of enemy ships. None of them were in any doubt now that victory could not be had there today.

"Put me through to the Commodore," said Ryan.

Clark's face came up on a screen projection beside that of the ensuing battle.

"Sir, we can't stay here. Much longer and they'll roll over us," stated Ryan.

"Our orders are to defend this location at all costs, Captain. At all costs! You do your duty, Clark out."

The screen cut off, and Ryan was left with an even more bitter taste in his mouth than that caused by the fumes of the recent fires.

"Sir, we've got incoming assault pods!"

Ryan looked to the screen at the small craft rushing for their position, far smaller than the large rams that had crashed into the Collingwood. They could carry just five to ten Mechs each, but they were still every bit as terrifying.

"Shoot the bastards down. We can't let them get aboard!"

The Deveron's guns raged at the wing of drop pods heading their way. The first salvo destroyed four outright, but another half a dozen were still closing. The rapid speed at which they approached only gave enough time for one more rushed salvo. Three of the pods smashed into the hull of the Deveron.

"This is Ryan to Samson. We have multiple hull breaches."

"On it, Sir," he quickly replied over their comms.

Small explosions erupted throughout the ship as the enemy blasted the rest of their way onboard. Ryan turned to look at the entrance to the bridge, half expecting to see the Mechs stomping towards him. The marines stood confidently at the doorway with their weapons at the ready, but the navy crew were terrified. Most had forgotten the rest of the battle altogether. Coming face-to-face with a Mech was something that should be feared, but Ryan knew he must face their other troubles. He snapped around.

"Lieutenant! Give me an update on the enemy progress."

There was silence for a moment as Wayans got back to his screens.

"Sir, we've got enemy cruisers almost on top of us. There ain't much left of the minefield. The Collingwood says she's still in the fight, but see for yourself, Sir."

He panned their display screen around to show the flagship. Fires raged along her length, and enemy pulses continued to hammer the hull.

"God knows how many Mechs they have aboard."

Gunfire burst out behind them, the heavy calibre marine rifles echoing around the bridge, causing them all to flinch.

"They're here," Ryan said to himself.

He lifted his rifle and rushed to the door where the marines were firing.

"How have they got this close?" he asked.

"Sir, it's a big ship for a few dozen marines to cover. That's why we're here," replied Corporal Herrera.

Ryan stuck his head out from a barricade they had setup. The bodies of two Mechs were in the corridor. More fire could be heard faintly from further back in the Deveron.

"Sir, we just lost half our starboard weapons!"

"What?"

"They're being blown from the inside, Sir."

The Marine corporal beside him leaned in.

"Same as we'd do if we could. Without our guns, they'll blow us out of the sky in no time."

There is no sky here, thought Ryan. *Run or die.*

He spun around and shouted at Wayans.

"Get me Clark, right now!"

He rose to his feet and strode across the bridge as the comms channel opened. The Commodore was looking calm, but they could all hear the gunfire not so far away.

"Sir, we can't stay in this fight any longer!"

"We can and we will, Captain."

"Damn it, Sir, we can do no further good here. We'll lose this fleet for nothing gained. We've done all the damage we can to those bastards."

"And so you just want to let them roll on to Earth?"

"We don't have a choice, anymore! All we can do is retreat and re-group with the rest of our fleets so we have a fighting chance."

"I will not abandon this position!"

An explosion erupted behind the Commodore, and debris tumbled down over his head. In the ensuing chaos, they could only watch as pulses and gunfire were traded across the bridge of their flagship. The feed stayed open, and they could see marines pushing their way across the bridge, their officer shouting at the crew.

"Get us the hell out of here!"

One of the Navy officers appeared before them where the Commodore had previously stood. Blood trickled down the woman's face, and fear had almost overcome her.

"This is the Collingwood. Initiate immediate withdrawal. Get back to Earth anyway you can!"

Further explosions erupted, and the signal was cut off, but they could already see the flagship's engines roar to life. Whoever was left alive was getting out of there with all haste.

"Get moving, now!" yelled Ryan.

Wayans was already ahead of him. They had been anticipating the order from the second they first saw the enemy.

"Herrera, get to those starboard gun positions, and take down whatever bastards are there!"

"Sir, I have orders to hold the bridge."

"If we don't deal with whatever got aboard, we could lose weapons, or God forbid, engines, at any moment. We've got the bridge. You take the fight to them!"

"Yes, Sir."

Ryan could see the look of glee in the marine's eyes. After seeing from the bridge of the Deveronthe vicious mauling the fleet had received,he wanted nothing more than to get his pound of flesh.

"On me, now!" he ordered.

The five of them rushed out with determination to crush all before them. Ryan turned to his bridge crew.

"All I need right now is a pilot and gunner. The rest of you guard that doorway."

Despite the horrifying prospect of what it might entail,

no one contested the order. They were still in shock from the vicious attack but relieved to be leaving the enemy behind. As they got out of hearing distance, Wayans finally spoke.

"Sir, you think we can escape from them?"

"They'll be licking their wounds for a while, and they ain't any quicker than us these days," Ryan replied proudly.

He turned to the display screen. Four of the eleven ships had been left behind. Two were nothing more than floating hulks, and the other two were quickly following suit.

"I hope they met a quick and painless end," stated Wayans.

Ryan nodded in agreement, but he knew many of them would not have received such mercy. Gunfire still poured from the Deveron at the enemy ships, but they were quickly reaching the limits of their range. The enemy fighters were gone now, but the largest enemy guns still harassed them.

"The Collingwood looks in a bad way."

"They're still moving," replied Ryan. There's a lot to be said for that."

"Sir, we got incoming!"

Before he could turn, a pulse smashed into the defences at the door to the bridge. The crew ducked down behind it as fragments of the pulse splintered out across the deck. Ryan could smell the burn of the pulse fragments eating into their metal deck. Further pulses continued to hit the position where the crew were hunkered down. No one wanted to stick his neck out to return fire.

"Put some fire down on them!" he shouted.

They heard his order but didn't respond. They were frozen by the fear of impending death as the creatures stomped up the corridor towards them. Between the cracking bursts of pulses, they could hear the steps getting nearer. Ryan cursed as he leapt to their position and slammed up against the edge of the doorway.

"The only thing that's going to stop them is us, now start shooting!"

He leaned around the corner and let off a burst from his rifle. There was little need to aim, as the corridor was relatively narrow and straight. He caught a glimpse of at least two creatures before a pulse racing towards his head made him jerk back. The impact ripped a half a metre hole in the edge of the doorway. The blast impact barely missed the Captain.

Wayans look around in panic. His back faced the doorway from his seat, but he could not leave his post. Ryan leaned into the hole that had been blasted and fired another burst. It was enough to inspire the others to do the same. Dozens of rounds were thrown down the corridor, but few were aimed shots.

Ryan ducked back again, but when he leaned around for another attempt, he felt the heat of the enemy's weapon as a pulse fired. He stopped just in time to save himself, but he knew the enemy were right on top of them. He held is rifle around the corner and blind fired the rest of his magazine, jumping back to put in another. As he did so, he looked up to see his scared comrades hiding.

"Get up there and shoot!"

He pushed in the new mag and turned into the doorway once again. He suspected it would be his last and opened up on full auto. He had a full view of the creatures now, and his rounds smashed into the nearest one, killing it quickly. But two others were close behind. They're weapons quickly powered up and were about to unleash a fury of pulses when an explosion erupted behind them, sending them crashing to the deck.

The crew watched in shock and delight as marines rushed up the corridor, firing rapidly at the wounded creatures until they stood over their vanquished foes and made sure the job was finished. Lieutenant Samson was at the head of the marines. His armour was scorched and clothing of his upper right arm burnt from an enemy pulse, but he seemed unaffected by it.

"Where are we up to, Captain?" he asked, as if nothing had changed.

"Fleet is bugging out. We're overrun."

"No shit," he responded.

"Have you cleared all those bastards out yet?"

Before Samson could answer, a few gunshots rang out

where they had come from.

"We're flushing the last of them out as we speak."

Ryan nodded in acknowledgement. He could see the marine was maintaining his position at the bridge until the ordeal was over, and Ryan wasn't going to complain. The two of them turned to look at the viewing screens that now showed their flanks and stern. Shots still poured back from where they'd left, but in less number now. Samson gasped at the sight of the damage of the larger vessels around them.

"We could never have held there with so small a force," he stated.

"No, we couldn't. But neither did they come out of the fight unscathed."

"Sir, if I may ask. Why the hell were we just a bare bones operation when such a threat was ever present?"

Ryan sighed as he thought it over.

"People wanted to believe it was all over. We were just a token force."

"They won't believe it now."

Ryan turned back to Wayans and could see the relief in his face. Many of the crew were still huddled behind cover with their rifles clenched to their bodies. Ryan knew they had come within minutes of losing the lives of everyone in the fleet.

"Any sign of them following us?" he asked.

"Negative, Sir, or not at any speed anyway."

The Captain breathed out in relief and could see the rest of the crew relax. He thought they had been posted to a lifeless and deathly boring tour at the Gateway, but now they faced another war and were running for their lives.

"Won't they ever leave our System alone?" asked Wayans.

"Nope, not while we fight to defend it."

CHAPTER TWO

"What are their intentions? What are they coming for? How can they be stopped?" These are the questions we must all ask and get answers to," said General White. "Let us remember that this is an emergency meeting. We have little information but must make quick decisions."

The room was silent for a moment as over thirty high-ranking military officials from the major powers in the World discussed the news. Most were projected through screens placed around the table. Only five sat in the room from where White hosted the talks.

"The Secretary of Defence has left this in my hands to discuss and take the appropriate measures once we, as a collective, can make a decision."

Finally Field Marshal Copley spoke up.

"Seems to me that we need information more than anything. We must gather our forces at Earth while scouts are sent out to find out what the hell is going on, and what is bearing down on us."

"Are we here yet again? Ready to fight to the death once more for no reason?" asked Dupont.

White shook his head in disbelief. He had quickly come to understand how Taylor had come to blows with the idiot of a General.

"The simple facts are this, General. We have a fight coming our way. That shouldn't be such a surprise anymore. We can wait for them to come to us and have no information at all. Or we can send out intelligence gatherers so that we better understand our position."

"And those are our only two options?" Dupont replied sharply.

"Clearly they are," Schulz said.

Dupont had his nose put out of place by the German officer, but he could do little but accept it as Schulz continued.

"We have a fleet like never before. Clearly Commodore Clark managed to put up a fight against the enemy with what little he had. I propose we prepare the fleets for immediate action while information is gathered through scouting parties."

"Okay, then we are in agreement. As you are all aware, Colonel Taylor has a turncoat that joined him some way back. That defector has proven to be more than useful and trustworthy. Taylor's unit is presently training

MDF forces on the Moon. I can have him dispatched immediately. Between them, they are our best hope of reliable information."

Out of the corner of his eye, the General could see Dupont curse at the name of the Colonel. That tickled him a little, as he already hated the Frenchman.

"We should send another four scouting parties alongside him. Each aboard different ships, the fastest we have. We need to know everything we can," General Richards added.

"Then it is decided. We have many dark days ahead, but we have seen it all before. Seen it, fought it, beaten it. Let's make sure all our people know we're on the winning side."

* * *

"Second team go!" shouted Taylor.

Soldiers rushed from cover past the Colonel and Commander Kelly who stood watching. A platoon of his Inter-Allied was opposing the MDF in a training exercise.

"An enemy ship has breached your perimeter, and your guys have just a minute or two to contain them before they run rampant," Taylor said.

"I don't think any of us need reminding of it," he replied.

Shouts rang out as the MDF soldiers advanced and laid down fire. The blank ammunition was every bit as loud as the real thing, and the laser tag devices fitted ensured they had the correct effect.

The two officers watched as a hundred MDF soldiers closed in on their target. They all utilised the Reitech equipment that Taylor had become so accustomed to.

"It's a God damn miracle we're even still alive to be training for this," Kelly said.

"Amen to that," he replied.

Buzzers went off in the distance as the lasers tagged the opposition. The battle was out of sight now as the close quarter battle continued in the distance. Fifteen minutes later the shots finally stopped.

"Clear!"

Taylor lifted his comms device.

"Training exercise complete. Well done, return to the rally point."

The troops began to flood back down the corridor past them. Jafar was among them and could be seen many ranks down due to his towering presence.

"That's not a sight I'm ever going to get used to, one of them in our uniform," Kelly.

"I used to think the same, but I'll never say never after the shit I've seen."

Kelly smiled and nodded in agreement. Jafar now wore sergeant stripes upon his armour and was directly attached to Taylor's command staff. The alien had become good friends with Silva while learning everything he could from the Sergeant Major.

"Colonel, I'd have you and your command staff dine with me tonight."

"It would be an honour," replied Taylor.

"I'll see you there, Colonel."

* * *

Taylor stepped into the officer's quarters he had been provided and could already tell Eli was occupying the place. Her gear was scattered over the desk, and the shower was on. He knew she couldn't have been there long, as the water restrictions only allowed the showers to run for up to two minutes every twelve hours. That was considered adequate for a single occupant.

The door closed behind him, and the shower turned off moments later. She was clearly aware of his presence. She stepped out of the bathroom with a cheeky smile on her face.

"You know that'll be all the water I get for hours."

"Ah, you don't need it, Colonel. You've stood around watching all day while the rest of us sweat."

He could do nothing but smile. He had been looking forward to getting cleaned up, but the sight of her was so much more appealing.

"So the Commander has invited you to dinner?"

"Yep, sure has."

"Damn, bet you'll be getting some good food."

"Bet your ass."

"Don't fancy taking a date?"

Taylor shook his head.

"We may just about get away with carrying on like this, but if we flaunt it before those around us, it'll only bring trouble."

"And what would they do to the great Colonel Mitch Taylor. Leader of the Immortals, slayer of Karadag?"

"Hey, you're not the one who spent a few months in the brig. I can do without that experience again."

He pulled of his BDUs and threw them down over Parker's gear. The room was a mess, but he figured he couldn't make it any worse. There was just enough water left to wash his face.

"That food tonight will better than the shit we get."

"Privileges of rank," he replied with a smile.

Mitch pulled out his service dress from the wardrobe. It was the only other uniform he had with him, and the smartest thing he could manage. He figured evening dress would be too much for Kelly anyway, who was a man of simple tastes. As he tried to get dressed, Eli did her utmost to stop him. She wrapped her arms around his shoulders and tried to entice him to stay.

"Come on, you know Kelly can't withstand lateness."

She let go and slumped down on the bed with a sigh and curse.

"Is this all our lives are now? One training exercise to another on base after base?"

"We're in the Corps. Our lives are what we are told. Another few weeks and we'll get our leave. We can head for Monterey and soak up the sun. Down cocktails to our hearts content and be the layabouts you fancy us to be."

"Mmm, sounds good. I'll believe it when I see it."

He made the final adjustments to his tie in the mirror, looking down at her glum face.

"Hey come on. This is luxury compared to the times we have known, a real bed, regular sleep, and nobody trying to kill us. I'll only be a few hours."

"I'll be waiting."

It was a short walk to Kelly's home, an apartment atop one of the towers of the colony. Two MDF soldiersposted at the door ushered him inside. It struck Taylor as strange that he would have a protection detail at his personal residence.

The Colonel made his way though into the penthouse. It opened up into a lavish open plan environment that was prime real estate on the Lunar colony. It didn't feel like the kind of place Kelly would have chosen. Taylor could only suspect it came along with the job. Up ahead, he could hear a hive of conversation, and he caught the last few comments.

"How long have we got till the bastards get here?" asked one officer.

Taylor's face turned to stone as he'd already anticipated the subject of the conversation. He pushed his way through two officers. There were over a dozen MDF officers stood about talking.

"Until which bastards get here?" he asked sternly.

The room fell silent as he strode in between them. His eyes contacted with Kelly, and he could see the weariness on the Commander's face.

"They're back, those alien bastards."

Taylor was silent. He always expected them to return, but it was no less shocking.

"What do you know so far?"

Kelly took in a deep breath, as if to prepare for the passing on of such dire news.

"Not an awful lot at present. The Collingwood and what is left of the SGD, that's the Space Gateway Defence, is in full retreat. They've lost four or five vessels and are doing running repairs while making their way here with all haste."

"The Deveron was out there. Did she make it out?"

"She did indeed, and is on her way here, right now."

"How are we just hearing about this?"

"The SGD centre has only known for the last twenty-four hours. Colonel, I have been informed of your orders and told to relay them to you presently."

Taylor expected the Commander to usher him into some more private quarters, but he laid it out for all to hear.

"The Deveron will be here within hours. You are to take what elements of the Inter-Allied are here and report to her for immediate departure. Your task is to gather any information you can on what's heading our way."

A few of the officers gasped and sniggered at the order.

"Sir? Head towards them, with one ship?"

"Four other vessels are being sent out on similar information gathering missions. The honest truth is your eyes, and that of your alien friend, are what's needed. Get out there, gather any info you think could be useful, and get back safely. The fleet will be waiting for you when you haul ass back here."

"Better be, Sir, because we'll be coming in hot."

"Now, the rest of you. The last time we faced unbeatable odds, we chose to stay and defend our homes without knowing what we had let ourselves in for. I will not make the same mistake again. The colony is what it is because of the people who inhabit it. I am ordering an immediate evacuation to Earth."

There was no argument from the officers present. Several had fought for their survival on the Moon, and none wanted to go through it again. Kelly turned to Taylor.

"You haven't got long, Colonel. Gather your people and be ready. She'll be docking at platform seven. Good luck to you."

"And to you, Sir."

Taylor rushed out of the room and immediately lifted his comms unit.

"2nd Inter-Allied. Grab your gear and report to platform seven. We are leaving."

He didn't want to say anything else across open channels, but he knew they would already suspect a major problem coming their way. There would be no other reason for them to leave their training mission for anything but an emergency. He reached his quarters and found Parker inside, almost ready to go.

"What the hell's up?" she asked.

"Hell? Exactly that, coming our way and fast."

She tilted her head and stared at his face to see if he really meant what she suspected. He could see exactly what she was thinking and asking with her eyes.

"Yep, it's exactly that."

"Christ!"

He ripped of his service dress and tossed it into his kit bag. He knew he wouldn't have any need for it for a long time.

"We rendezvousing with the rest of the fleet?"

He ignored the comment and continued to get into his BDUs.

"Mitch?" she asked.

He knew she wasn't going to leave it alone.

"We're heading out in the Deveron on recon."

She shook her head in disbelief.

"What?" he asked.

"Nothing... just that why do we always get the shit jobs?"

"Well in this case, I can honestly say we are in the wrong place at the wrong time. Being here on the Moon right now, and having Jafar's knowledge and counsel, means we were perfect for this."

"Great, I'll remind you of that when we're up to our necks in shit."

Taylor could do nothing but smile in response. She was more beautiful than ever when she was angry. She could see that in his face, and it only made her more furious.

* * *

The thirty-six marines of Inter-Allied lay about the docking bay awaiting their ride as the colony erupted into organised chaos. The evacuation had begun, and nobody was in any doubt as to what was coming their way. Taylor could only watch and wish the human fleet had been so substantial when it all began. Leaving the colony with the Prime Minister while the battle raged was a memory he would never forget, and one of the lowest points in his career.

Taylor had explained to all who were with him what their mission was. There had not been a single question or discussion about it. They were somehow numbed by the news, but he had spent the last year preparing them for it. It wasn't long before the Deveron arrived. The ramp lowered, and Taylor rushed forward to greet Ryan with excitement but was met by a grim sight.

Captain Ryan stepped out at the head of a line of stretcher-bearers. Five dead were carried out, and three walking wounded followed.

"Attention on deck!"

The call came from Jafar and was immediately responded to. It was the first time he had ever done as such, and Taylor was impressed with his perception on the situation. He was showing the respect to their fallen like one of his own. There were still some who didn't trust the alien, but he counted Jafar among his closest friends.

The wounded passed, and Taylor could see three of the dead were marines. Ryan approached and stopped before him with a salute. Taylor tried to find the words to say, but nothing seemed appropriate.

"You weren't wrong, Colonel. You always said the bastards would be back, and they are, and stronger than ever."

"Any idea on the numbers we face?"

"Honestly, they just kept coming. It didn't matter how many we killed, how many ships we destroyed. They kept pouring through the Gateway and bearing down on us till there was nothing we could do but run. We barely made it out alive. Some weren't so lucky."

Mitch hated having to ask it, but he needed the Deveron and her crew back in action.

"Are you aware of your orders?"

"To take you back out there to gather intel."

It was a relief to not have to be the one to tell him.

"You got it. I am sorry there is no time to see to your casualties, but time is not on our side."

"Got it, Sir, mount up when you're ready."

Ryan's crew passed the casualties over to an MDF medical team, who had been awaiting their arrival, and quickly scrambled back aboard.

"Load up!" yelled Taylor.

A Marine Lieutenant waited at the ramp to the ship. Taylor could see the wound on his arm and the quick patch up that had been done. His armour was still scorched from the battle, but he didn't show any sign of it affecting his ability.

"Lieutenant Samson, Sir. I have been assigned as Marine detail to the Deveron."

"Colonel Taylor, 2nd Inter-Allied."

"I am well aware who you are, Sir. I can't think of a marine alive who wouldn't know your face."

Taylor smiled back. Samson seemed completely calm and unfazed by the battle he had so recently faced. It was clear he was a marine with plenty of combat experience.

"Welcome aboard, Colonel."

Taylor looked up at the hull of the Deveron one last

time and stepped inside. It felt good to be back aboard, but the battle scars were more present than ever. Blue blood trailed down one of the corridors where the body of a Mech had been dragged away. Metal support beams were twisted and burnt. Crews were busy cutting and welding on multiple levels to repair the damage. Samson stepped through to escort the Colonel to the bridge.

"Looks like you had a hell of a fight to get out of there."

"Just what we have come to expect of the Mechs, Sir. The surprise was seeing them again. All in all, we did well to get out of there with so few lost, but a minute longer, and I don't think any of us would have made it."

Taylor shook his head.

"I've been telling our Commanders for the last year that this would happen. How can anyone have been so stupid to assume they would just leave us alone?"

"Well, looks like your wish has come true."

"Mmm, can't say I wanted them to come, but we do have some unfinished business."

"This is the Captain speaking. We lift off in sixty seconds."

The two officers reached the bridge that felt like home to Taylor. Those who knew him and the fresher faces greeted him, but there was little enthusiasm in their faces. Taylor sat down at one of the workstations. He wouldn't lie about in anyone else's vessel, but the Deveron was an exception. A few seconds later, Ryan strode onto the deck.

He was young for the Captain of such a vessel; and as aresult of the war that he would not have desired.

"Liftoff in five, four, three..."

The engines roared, and the Deveron quickly lifted from the docking bay. Within seconds, Wayans was putting full power down, and they soared out into space. After clearing the docking bays, they could see the extent of the evacuation. War ships, cargo liners, and civilian ships were all working together to take every human being from the Moon to safety. Taylor looked out at the defence grip around Earth. It was an impressive installation, but he still wasn't convinced it would be all that so many hoped for.

"When we fled, their fleet didn't seem to be following us with any haste. I guess we have a good few days yet before they reach us, maybe a week or more."

"Why would they do that?" asked Taylor.

"Only reason I know of is if they have brought the Gezgen K'til."

"The what?"

"The Planet Killer."

Taylor suddenly leapt to his feet and turned to the face the alien.

"How is it this is the first we are hearing of it?"

"I have not seen it in seventy of your years. I never thought I would again. The last time I was just young. It was returning from a great victory."

"Seventy years ago? How old are you?" Ryan asked.

"Eighty-three years. The Krycenaean can easily live to twice what a human does."

"Not with a bullet in their head, they don't," replied Samson.

Taylor nodded in agreement. But just as he smiled at the comment, he was reminded of the original topic.

"This Planet Killer. It may sound like a stupid question, but what is it?"

The bridge was silent as everyone's attention turned to Jafar. Not even the pilot Wayans could turn away.

"All I know is that when used it kills all life on a planet and renders that planet uninhabitable to even us for a long time."

"How long?"

"A hundred years, two hundred maybe."

Gasps echoed around the room. Taylor turned to Samson.

"Log everything we have just heard, and ensure it is sent directly to General White within the hour."

"Aye, aye, Sir."

The Lieutenant sat down at the nearest workstation and immediately got to work. He knew more was likely to be spoken in the next few minutes, and he could not afford to miss anything from his transmission. Taylor sat back down, trying to comprehend what that meant for all of them. Everyone waited for him to speak as they reflected on the same words.

"You told me they thought of Earth as a paradise, so why would they destroy it?"

"Either they don't think they can win, or someone is seriously pissed off," replied Ryan.

Taylor nodded in agreement.

"The Gezgen K'til won't destroy Earth. It will just delay its occupation. I never thought I would see it brought here though. Demiran's family built the monster two hundred years ago."

"Demiran? Your former boss and the one we captured?"

Jafar nodded.

"Well, that's just fucking great. He must be pissed."

"Can this Gezgen, whatever it is, be stopped?"

" The Gezgen K'til is a massive ship. The same class as what you called Tartaros in the first war. I know it must get close to the planet to operate, as the last time it was used, a great battle had to be fought above the planet before it could be deployed."

"So this was used against another race?" asked Ryan.

"That doesn't matter, right now. Let's concern ourselves with our own world," replied Taylor. "So what you're saying is this. If that thing can get to the atmosphere of Earth, our planet is gone for our lifetimes!"

Jafar nodded.

"Christ. We need confirmation of this. Samson. Include all the information you have heard, but make it clear that the presence of this Planet Killer is still just a theory."

The bridge fell silent again as they considered the possibility of losing Earth, and more urgently that they were heading straight for the Planet Killer.

"You've all had a long day. My marines will take on any watches they can. Everyone not on duty get some rest. We've got a hell of a time ahead of us."

* * *

Two days passed without any contact when Taylor was awoken in the middle of the night Earth time. He pulled on his Reitech gear and rushed to the bridge to find the crew standing frozen and staring at the display screen.

"There's your visual confirmation, Colonel," Ryan said.

Taylor turned to Jafar to ask if it was what he had suspected. Before he could say a word, the alien nodded to pre-empt him. Taylor looked back at the screen. He could not tell it and Tartaros apart, but he trusted his friend. They looked out at the hundreds of support ships escorting the behemoth.

"Doesn't make any sense," Taylor murmured.

"What?" Ryan asked.

"The strength of their forces. Why didn't they send all this through to begin with? With all of this, and what they sent in the first war, we would have been crushed in the beginning. Before we had time to learn from their technology and stop them."

Nobody answered until Taylor turned to Jafar for answers.

"Well?"

"The Krycenaean people are not as one, under one rule. Powerful leaders rule factions and planets. Each wants his own glory and power. They rarely stand beside eachother. Demiran would almost never stand beside Karadag, but he would make every effort to avenge him for his own gains."

"So there is no one leader?" asked Taylor.

"One who is more powerful than the other Lords, one who holds more influence than the rest, but not with the control over all the others you would think."

"And this boss, who is he?"

"Erdogan. The strongest, cruellest, and most power hungry of the Krycenaean Lords."

"Then you have met him?"

"I have seen him. As a personal guard to Demiran, I met him once, but he would not know me."

"Well, this just keeps getting better. Are we ever likely to see this Erdogan?"

Jafar shrugged his shoulders.

"He could be aboard the Gezgen K'til. He might have even been on Earth during the first war. I don't know."

"But that is Demiran's ship, right?"

"Yes. Lord Erdogan can rightfully take his place aboard any ship in any war. He can take the glory without having to front the expense of using his own resources."

"I sure would like to get my hands on that bastard," said Parker.

It was the first thing she had said since Taylor had reached the bridge that morning. She had stayed so still and quiet that her presence had gone unnoticed.

"This big bad, the Erdogan. He must want Earth, right? Seems every other Krycenaean does."

"I don't know."

"All right. I've seen enough, and all this information is giving me a damn headache. Captain, collect as much data as you can, and then get us the hell out of here."

"Wait!" Jafar shouted.

Taylor snapped around. It was a surprise to have Jafar assert himself so much. He could see the alien pointing at the corner of a display screen. He turned and carefully studied what at first looked like empty space. Then his eyes widened as he caught a glimmer of movement. It was the flicker of the chameleon ship camouflage that Taylor had all but forgotten.

"They're onto us. Get us out of here!"

"No," replied Jafar, "right now, their guns are training on us. We'd not make it."

"Then what do we do?"

"This ship, the Deveron, it must be known to Demiran and many others. They would want whoever was aboard alive."

"Are you willing to bet money on that?"

"I don't have any money," Jafar replied dryly.

Taylor could not help smile for just a second.

"All right then. You seem to have an idea of what you're doing. Tell us what we should do."

They all looked to Jafar. Nobody aboard no longer doubted they could trust him, and he had the unique advantage of both his heritage and training by the Inter-Allied.

"There will be two of them out there, one on overwatch and one closing to board us. They're hoping to either board us with the element of surprise or destroy us if we try to run. Those are patrol ships. They have maybe fifty Mechs on board each of them."

"Shi...it," replied Samson.

"If they could have got aboard undetected, we'd be finished. But with a prepared defence, that's another story."

He stopped and thought for a moment about what Jafar had said.

"That one we saw closing to our starboard side must be the boarding action, right?"

Jafar nodded in response.

"Okay, I want all but a protection detail for the bridge to the starboard side and ready to repel borders. Captain, have your gun crews prepared to fire at the other ship, but do not show any sign of it until the last second."

"We don't even know where the other vessel is," he replied.

"They must put out a heat signature, however faint. Find it!"

"Why don't we just blast them now?" asked Parker.

"We need that other ship on overwatch to let its guard down. Right now, that crew is waiting with their fingers on the trigger to give us everything they have got. As soon as the other has boarded us, we should have an opening."

"Where will they breach?" asked Taylor.

"At the main hull door if they can."

"Right then, masks on for everyone. Once they get aboard, we give them hell. I'll give you the green light when to fire, Captain. When that is done, we need to get that other ship off us fast and make tracks. Parker, have charges ready to blow the breaching clamps. I don't want them hanging on any longer than we need them to."

"You got it, Sir."

She rushed off about her business.

"You all know what you have to do. Do not give the enemy any indication of our intentions. Don't even let anything slip over the comms, nothing until the firing starts. Let's go!"

He rushed to the starboard side and grabbed a shield from the racks where they were stored ready for such occasions. They were cumbersome and bulky things to lug around, but well worth it when the fighting started. He took a knee behind his shield and waited for the inevitable enemy breach. Parker positioned behind him with a crate full of magnetic explosives.

For a full minute nothing happened, and they all waited in silence, listening for the enemy presence. Finally, they heard the quiet and subtle clamps attach onto the Deveron. Had they not been ready for it, Taylor doubted anyone would have noticed until the doors were blown. They were coming through the main hull doors just as Jafar had said. Taylor looked over to the turncoat alien and nodded in appreciation for his knowledge and efforts.

Controlled charges blasted all around the door, sending it crashing into the bulkhead the other side of the room. It would have been ear splitting, were it not for the helmets they all wore. A fine cloud of dust swept out around them from the blast, and through it they could hear the footsteps of the Mechs rushing for the opening. Taylor held the comms unit on his sleeve close and whispered.

"Ryan, now."

Power surged in the ship as energy was sent immediately to the gun ports, and the ship rocked slightly with the initial salvo of everything they had.

"Fire!" yelled Taylor.

Twenty marines had a field of fire on the doorway. Nothing was getting through unscathed. The first four Mechs were killed instantly by multiple bursts of fire from the Reitech rifles. As they continued to fire, a big metal looking ball was launched in from the doorway and rolled into the middle of the room.

"Down!" cried Taylor.

He looked away and crouched down behind his shield just in time. The device erupted with a blinding burst of light and a blast that sent him off his feet. The shield was ripped from his grip as he was thrown against Parker. He staggered to get to his feet. Despite avoiding the worst of the blast and light, he was still stunned by the amount he had been subjected to.

Taylor sat up and could see several other marines lying unconscious or badly disorientated. He looked around, and a Mech stomped through the dust cloud. It lifted its rifle to fire at him. In a desperate attempt, Mitch reached for the shield and pulled it in front of him. Three pulses smashed into it. The last of which tore a hole through the centre, burning into the armour on his arm.

He let out a cry in pain as the pulse fragments burnt into his flesh, and what remained of the shield dropped to the deck. There was nothing left to save him. He was still too stunned to quickly get back to his feet. He hoped for a miracle, and it came. Jafar leapt onto the Mech, ripping the faceplate from its armour and clubbing its exposed head with the stock of his rifle until the skull fractured.

Jafar reached down and grabbed Taylor by the rim of his chest plate armour, hauling him to his feet as if he were a rag doll. Taylor just about managed to hold his body weight and grabbed the nearest rifle that had been blown across the room. Pulses and gunfire zipped from one side of the entrance hall to the ship to the other. He quickly recognised the shape of a Mech and began firing, despite his vision still being a little blurred.

Samson rushed in from the forward corridor with fresh troops and joined the fight. It was perfect timing, as the enemy was starting to make progress at getting into the ship. Six of Taylor's marines lay dead and several others wounded. Samson advanced with his unit with their shields held forward, laying down a wall of fire. More of Taylor's unit were regaining their composure and joining the fray. The Mechs visible in the entrance were smashed back and retreating into their ship. Taylor turned around to see if Eli was ready with the charges. She was getting to her feet with the crate in hand.

"Push them back! Parker, get your ass here!"

The marines advanced forward with Taylor and Jafar at the centre. They put down a wall of fire as their covered the ground until they reached the breach.

"Give 'em everything. I don't want them returning fire when we break!" Taylor ordered.

An extending corridor from the enemy ship connected the two ships, ten metres long and three Mechs wide. Parker took out the first few larger charges and punched in the timers before tossing them the length of the corridor. The last few smaller ones she placed at the nearest point.

"That's it! Everyone back!"

They rushed back as she lifted the trigger and pressed down with her thumb. The shaped charges produced a small controlled blast that cut the boarding corridor in two. The ships drifted apart. Just five seconds later, a blast erupted in the enemy ship, and it was torn apart. Taylor and Eli watched from the open breach in the Deveron.

"Jesus, how short did you set those timers?"

"Twenty seconds," she replied with a smile.

Taylor laughed.

"Hey, you said to be sure they wouldn't shoot back."

He slapped her on the shoulder.

"Nice work."

He lifted his comms unit.

"Ryan, get us the hell out of here!"

Before he'd finished the sentence, the engines were roaring at full power. Samson stepped up to the breach and breathed a sigh of relief.

"Close call," he whispered.

"As always. Get these wounded to medical. Parker, get engineering crews down here to patch it up."

He looked around to the wounded one last time.

This mission has cost us dearly just to confirm what we already suspected, he thought.

"Jafar, Your information was correct, but I wish to God it hadn't been. Walk with me."

They carried on back towards the bridge. As Taylor

threw his rifle over his shoulder, he was reminded of the pain in his arm. The thick Reiter designed armour only covered their torso. The rest of their armour was the same old stuff they had worn from the start and was only effective against minimal blast damage.

"That device they used cost us dearly. We must find a way to minimise its effects, but I fear we have much greater issues upon us."

"Demiran bringing the Gezgen K'til here can mean only thing."

Taylor was listening intently.

"That he has a bitter hatred running so deep for humanity that he would go to any length to end it."

"Why?"

Jafar shrugged his shoulders.

"I cannot think of any offence caused which would do as such. We have killed many of his soldiers, but that alone would not be enough. Either he is sick of the stubbornness of your race who refuse to quit, or he suffered more personally in the last battle in a way we do not know."

"When though?"

"We left Tau Ceti with Colonel Chandra still fighting. I don't know what could have happened or how, but something happened to Demiran then which has changed this war for him altogether."

CHAPTER THREE

Taylor sat gazing out of the window at the flagship Washington they were approaching. Rains was at the helm. It almost felt like the Lieutenant had become Taylor's personal pilot since it had all begun. The trail of vessels from the Moon had stopped now. He could only imagine the evacuation was complete. They had fled to Earth for safety, but he wondered how safe they really were.

"You ever seen such a grand fleet?" asked Eddie.

It was indeed something to marvel at. The combined human fleet was over three times the size of what set out for the fated Tau Ceti expedition. The Earth Defence Grid was equally as impressive; a chain of gun satellites and missile silos floating in orbit. Earth had become a fortress, and rightly so.

"Bloody fantastic," replied Taylor sarcastically.

"Hey, you don't want a chance to give those alien

bastards what for?"

Eddie turned back to look at Jafar sitting beside the Colonel.

"No offence," he added with a smile.

Jafar didn't respond to either comment. It was as if he didn't see himself as anything but human anymore. Within thirty minutes, the two of them were sitting in the officers' briefing room aboard the Washington. Key Naval and Marine officers sat around the vast conference table. Many empty places were filled with projection devices so that those on Earth could partake remotely.

Taylor laid out everything they had experienced and all the information they had learned from Jafar. He simply nodded in agreement with each statement. Admiral Huber was orchestrating the meeting and was the first to speak.

"This Planet Killer must obviously be stopped. That is not an option. We therefore have no choice but to engage the enemy in space. We cannot fight them on the land as before."

There were grumbles in agreement. Nobody could see an alternative.

"What strikes me here is that we still have a great many things to learn from you, Sergeant... Jafar. You would be far better stationed on the Washington, or even sent back to Earth to assist with our intelligence gathering and understanding of the enemy."

Jafar shook his head.

"We could order you to do as such."

"And I would refuse. My brother and I allied ourselves to Colonel Taylor and gave our word to protect him. I cannot perform that duty anywhere else."

"You're in the Marine Corps now," spat Vega.

"Yes, with a responsibility to my fellow marines. I will not leave Inter-Allied or cease to serve the Colonel through any means but my death."

Vega opened his mouth to continue, but Huber stopped him.

"Captain, it seems to me that these are exceptional circumstances. The Sergeant has proven invaluable to us in the field and continues to provide vital intelligence from his current position. As a member of the fleet, he can carry out all that is required of him. Jafar has taken a leap of faith for us. Let us do the same for him."

"Thank you, Admiral," replied Taylor.

"Is that what you desire?" asked Huber.

"Yes. I am a warrior. All I know is how to fight, and that is what I will do."

"Okay, then tell us what we can expect from the fleet which is bearing down on us."

Everyone in the room had their attention on Jafar. Many had never seen an alien with their own eyes before, and yet now they were fixated on one.

"To Lord Demiran, the Gezgen K'til is everything. It is the unique feature of his family and their reputation. It is his symbol of power and control among the other Lords. It would also be impossible to replace. The Gezgen K'til will not be an easy target to strike. It will be preceded by a wave of far smaller ships. Skirmishers if you like. But these ships, they are a power unto themselves. If you want a shot at the Gezgen K'til, you must destroy them quickly, before the Planet Killer reaches Earth. If you do not, you will never withstand the onslaught of their combined power."

"How many ships are we talking about?"

"I grew up on stories of the Gezgen K'til. I have never seen it being used. From my knowledge, I would expect ten to twelve cruisers, of which I have encountered. They are collectively known as The Purge, and will carve their way through everything in their path to make way for the Gezgen K'til."

"Then we should make an impassable wall with our fleet," stated Vega.

"No, you will not stop them. Not like that. They will smash through anything. You cannot use a barrier defence. You need a tiered defence. Allow them through a weak frontline and funnel them into a gauntlet of mines and warships."

"We are familiar with the strategy," replied Huber. "One that has been employed many time in our history."

"For their size, their armour is thicker than anything you have ever seen. Reinforced prows to cut through other ships and reinforced hulls with their bridge at the core, much like this ship. They are almost unstoppable."

"Then how do we stop them?"

The only weakness of The Purge vessels is that they have few crew. Their massively thick armour compromises them in that way. Each ship is crewed by just thirty or forty. If you can get near them, and breach with marines, they are finished."

"Sounds like the exact opposite of what anyone would expect to do. You see something like that and you keep your distance," replied Huber.

Jafar nodded in agreement.

"How can marine parties get so close if they are so heavily armed?" asked Taylor.

"The Purge does not consider fighters and smaller craft a threat. They have relatively little defence against such."

"Maybe that's for a good reason," replied Huber.

"Yes, it is true that the hull of these vessels is almost impossible to breach. However, I did once go aboard one in the fleet. They have only one weak point; one thin point in their armour, the Captain's quarters. A view out into space is a valuable thing, and something no Krycenaean would go without."

"Why don't we just hit that point with our guns?" asked Vega.

"Because in itself the area holds no importance in combat. A breach there will do nothing to slow the cruisers down, nor cause any damage to the crew who will be deep in the belly of the ship. But breached at that point, marines would be able to blast their way further in."

"Mmm, so through their own vanity they present a weakness," replied Huber.

He turned to Taylor.

"What do you think, Colonel?"

Taylor was taken aback. He knew why they addressed so many questions to Jafar, but he was just another marine in the fleet.

"Sounds like a job the Corps will happily see to the end, Admiral."

"Latest reports suggest we have just twenty-four hours before their fleet reaches us."

"The Purge will be ahead of the rest of the fleet, which you can expect within an hour of their arrival."

"Doesn't give us a whole lot of time to get them out of the way. It seems to me they are sent as a diversion to make way for this Planet Killer, and we are actively seeking to be diverted by it," stated Huber.

"Sir, if I may," replied Taylor. "Nothing of what Jafar has told us has ever been anything but spot on. If he says this is the way it should be done, I believe him, and would be willing to put the full backing of the 2nd Inter-Allied behind him."

"That is high praise indeed."

The room fell silent for a moment. Taylor could see

they were all looking to the Admiral to make the decision.

"Colonel, I have almost a hundred and fifty ships at my disposal, but the lion's share must inevitably remain with the defence grid here for the defence of Earth. I will give you thirty to advance a hundred kilometres and attempt to make this plan work. Vice Admiral Bailey will command this enterprise from the Neptune."

Huber pointed to the Admiral, but Taylor was already well aware of who the Admiral was; a woman newly appointed to the roll and who had served throughout the war. She had done her job well, but not yet with distinction.

"I will give you everything you need to make this mission work, Colonel, but know that every ship we have is needed for the defence of Earth. I don't want to compromise anymore ships and personnel than is necessary to get the job done."

"Understood, Ma'am."

"Good. The rest of your Battalion is awaiting you aboard transports. I'll have them despatched to rendezvous with the Neptune immediately. From now on, I will be concerning myself with defence of Earth from here. You and Admiral Bailey have complete control over the operation to take on this Purge fleet," said Huber.

That's no small ask, thought Taylor.

"We have much more to discuss here. Bailey, Taylor, you have a big task ahead of you and little time."

The two rose from their seats and left the room with

Jafar close behind. Bailey spoke as soon as they were out into the corridor.

"Seems to me what you need from the Navy is a deep defensive column that will put down as much chaos and confusion as possible while you get your thing done."

"Yes, Ma'am."

"Then I'll leave you to make your plans. All I'll need to know is timings and flight paths, in order to give you clear runs at the Purge ships and fighter support to go with it. Let me know when you have it planned out. You have two hours. I'll see you aboard the Neptune, Colonel."

She split of from the two of them with her own escort. Taylor stopped for a moment and stared into Jafar's eyes.

"You really think this plan can work?"

"It has to. It will take Huber's fleet hours to get the better of the Purge. In that time, the Gezgen K'til could be in position,and it would be over for us all."

Taylor gestured for Jafar to follow him as they made their way back to Rains' ship.

"Say we can pull this off and get marines aboard every one of these Purge ships, what then? Set charges and blow them sky high?"

"I was, as you say, going to think outside the box."

"Go on."

"The Purge ships are heavily armoured, even by Krycenaean standards. Why not use them against the enemy? Destroying them would be advantageous. But we could use them to our advantage."

"Yes, yes. Load 'em with nukes and send them right into the Planet Killer."

Jafar nodded.

"Do you think it could work?"

"If we can take them, yes. The ship commands will have to be input from the bridge of each ship individually after they are taken. I can create a command string which will make it quick and simple for each team."

"Sounds crazy but might work."

Taylor couldn't believe what was being suggested, but their entire situation was beyond belief.

"It's a simple plan, but if we can make the first stage work, why not? I hope you're right about boarding these things."

They reached the ship. It was already waiting with the engines fired up and ready to go. They lifted off the second they had gotten through the door and before they'd found a seat.

"Everything in order, Colonel?" asked Rains.

"You ready for the craziest mission you ever heard of?" asked Taylor.

"After the shit we've been through, nothing would surprise me. Does it involve sticking it to the bastards?"

"Damn straight," replied Taylor.

"Well all right then, let's get this show on the move!"

* * *

Taylor strode into the temporary briefing room he'd been allocated aboard the Collingwood. All the key officers of 2nd Inter-Allied were gathered, along with Silva and Parker. All stood upon his arrival. He palmed them off as if embarrassed by the sentiment.

"Be seated!"

It took just ten minutes to explain the plan to them. They did not question it nor seem at all surprised.

"I am assigned a single platoon to the task of taking on the task of each ship in this Purge fleet. I know that spreads us thin. However, with the element of surprise, it should be all that is required to get the job done. It will also leave us a few platoons in reserve which will fill any holes if they arise."

"You mean if we get blown out of the sky on the way to the target?" asked Jackson.

For a moment Taylor was concerned the Captain doubted their mission, but Taylor could see the sarcasm in the Captain's face.

"I'm not saying this isn't a dangerous mission, but when have we ever known any other kind? This Purge must be stopped. I can't say I'm enthused about having volunteered for the task, but if you want something done right and all that."

A few laughs echoed around the room.

"As you all know, we have comms working again in spite of their jamming technology. This is a major breakthrough for us. When the battle begins, we will be hidden in the minefield and debris around it. This should easily conceal our craft until the last moment. Fighters from the Neptune and her support ships will provide further cover for our movements. Each assault craft will be allocated a target as they are identified. Lieutenant Ota, your Company will be the reserves for this. I pray you are not needed, but be ready for anything."

"Where will you be, Sir?" she responded.

"I will be with the first platoon to go in, with whoever volunteers for the job."

"I'll go!" replied Jones without hesitation.

Taylor thought for a moment. Risking a Company and Battalion commander in this first wave was a risky strategy, but he could see the confidence boost it gave to all who had heard it.

"Okay. Each platoon will be issued a command module that has been arranged by Jafar. The platoons must get in, neutralise all targets, deploy the command module, and arm a nuke before getting the hell out of there. Were this to involve a single ship, it would be a walk in the park. However, the logistics of this operation are such that timing must be impeccable. I will allocate each of you a target vessel before I begin the first assault. That could be the last communication you have from me once it all begins. Any questions?"

"How longer after this Purge fleet arrives can we expect the rest of the enemy?" asked Grey.

"From what we understand, it will be about an hour."

"Doesn't give us a whole lot of time to get this done," added Jackson.

"Nope, as always, time is not on our side. However, the element of surprise is. They may be coming for us, but we're gonna hit them in ways they could never have imagined. Anything else?"

"Assuming we get this done and get back off the cruisers, what then?" asked Jones.

"We return immediately to Bailey's fleet and join the rest of the fight."

"And if this fails?" asked Yorath.

"Be under no illusions. If this Planet Killer is able to fulfil its mission, it will be the end of Earth. Everyone on it will be dead, and it will be uninhabitable for centuries. If we cannot stop it, what remains of our fleet will be the last remnants of humanity."

Gasps and whispers filled the room and began to rise in volume.

"All right! Listen up. This is bad, and there is no doubt about that. But we can beat 'em, just like we have before."

"Sir, if this so called Purge fleet is so God damn important, why aren't we getting more resources to deal with it?" asked Jackson.

Taylor took in a deep breath and sighed. He felt just the same.

"The reality is we don't know a lot of intel on the enemy fleet or tactics beyond what Jafar has told us. Admiral Huber is understandably concerned about diverting too many of our forces away from the Planet Killer. There is a possibility that this Purge fleet is merely a distraction to make way for it, in which case we will handle that distraction. I want to turn that on its head and turn their own weapons on them."

"If we can take out this monstrosity, what else can we expect after it?" asked Jones.

Taylor nodded in agreement. *That's the kind of thinking I like.*

"That is a valid point. Right now we are concerned with the immediate catastrophic threat to Earth. Even if we succeed in our mission here, there will be no shortage of enemy to fight. The hope is we can do enough damage to break them here and drive them away."

"You think our Navy has that kind of power?" asked Ota.

"I think we have a hell of a chance, yeah. Whatever we do or don't have, the time has come, and we have to make it work."

They all went silent.

"Any other questions? Okay. You know what to do. Get to the boats. Everything you need will be issued at the docking bays. Make sure you have a full compliment of shields. They'll provide more than useful for this boarding action. Good luck to you all."

He stood up and left the room with Parker and Jafar trailing him.

"Permission to accompany you on the first assault?" she asked.

"Denied."

"Mitch?"

He stopped, turned to face her, and replied in a whisper.

"Look, what we choose to do in our own time is one thing, but we must stay professional in our jobs. You have a duty to your platoon. Be there for them like they are there for you."

"But..."

He lifted his hand and put his finger to her lips lightly to stop her.

"But nothing. I'll see you when it's all over. Report to your station, Sergeant."

She knew he was right, but it pained her to have to part from him once again.

"Aye, aye, Sir."

Taylor and Jafar arrived at the docking bay just in time to see the nuclear weapon being carried aboard. Rains stood with his arms crossed, watching with a smile. He looked immensely pleased with the new model craft he had so recently taken delivery of. It was a Stallion class, and despite the pristine body, he had already decorated it with a hand painted half naked lady.

"Woo hoo! Gonna blow some shit up today!" he yelled.

"Taylor smiled. Even in the face of apocalyptical destruction, the Lieutenant was his same cheery self.

"You know whatever pills you're taking sure would be popular right about now," replied Taylor.

"Oh, come on, Colonel, we're living exciting times! We're about to witness the biggest mothership of all time; big enough to kill every living thing on a planet. We're gonna see it, and then we're gonna blow it to hell!"

"That's certainly the plan. Have you been brought up to speed on what we are doing here?"

"We got it. Fly you in to breach the ships coming our way. All we got to do is deliver you safely and pull you out at the end."

"That about sums it up."

"Easiest thing in the world," replied Eddie with a wide grin.

Taylor lifted his arm to speak into his comms module.

"2nd Inter-Allied. Emplane immediately. Lift off in five."

Jones appeared at his side, ushering their platoon aboard. Among them were some of the Brits that had been with them from the very beginning. Monty and Blinker strode past, greeting the Colonel.

"Shame Colonel Chandra isn't here to see us blow the

bastards to hell, Sir," shouted Blinker.

Monty shook his head in shame.

"You remember her when you see the enemy again," replied Taylor.

"Sure will, Sir."

"Load up, Rains."

"You got it."

Taylor was the last aboard. The plan was set now, and all they could do was wait and hope the Purge fleet came as Jafar predicted. The alien was glued to his side throughout.

"Still confident about this plan?"

Jafar nodded.

"I served Demiran for many years. He is predictable. If he is using the Gezgen K'til, then he will do so in the exact manner it was used last and the times before that. No planet has stood against it and the Purge combined."

"Good to know," he replied sarcastically.

The ship lifted off within seconds of him sitting down behind Eddie and his co-pilot.

It gave the Colonel a sense of security to have Rains at the helm and keeping them safe. He had got them through hell many times before. He thought back on all the times they had survived against all odds.

I wonder how much longer our luck can hold out.

Jones could see the lost look in his eyes and quickly responded.

"Hey, it ain't all bad."

Taylor smiled cautiously.

"How'd you figure?"

"We're the Immortals, remember? Failure is not a possibility."

Taylor laughed.

"Whoever named us that can't have seen our casualty lists."

"Maybe it isn't important. It doesn't matter who lives and dies from the Immortals. Only that they struggle on, no matter what. Soldiers from around the World are spurred on by our victories. Their resolve holds because ours does."

"Mmm, but at hell of a cost. Isn't it time someone else took on the mantle?"

"We aren't the only ones fighting. I am sure plenty have had it just as bad."

Taylor nodded in agreement. He knew Jones to be correct, for he had seen the evidence with his own eyes. Thirty minutes later they were in position spread amongst the minefield before Bailey's fleet. The thirty ships she had were staggered into several lines of defence. To reach Earth via a direct path, the enemy would have to go right through them.

"You still sure they won't avoid us all together?" asked Jones.

"Positive. Demiran despises you and will accept nothing short of a full frontal attack. Anything that stands in his way must be crushed."

"Well, allright then. I sure hope you're right."

"He's not wrong," replied Rains.

"What is it?" asked Taylor.

"The Neptune has made visual contact."

"Put it on the display."

A projection came up front of them all. It wasas Jafar had described, hulking, heavily armoured vessels all matching. They had never seen such vessels before.

"Twelve of the bastards. Just as you said," said Jones.

"It's a good start," replied Taylor.

"Not sure that's how I'd describe it," Jones retorted.

"They're coming right for us. There's no doubt about it!" Eddie added.

"Strike two. It's going our way so far. How long till they reach the fleet?"

"They'll be in range in a few minutes," replied Eddie.

"Right, then it is a waiting game for us."

They did exactly that. The viewing screen was a projection from a camera aboard the Neptune. It was not long before the guns raged from both sides, but the enemy made no sign of slowing down. The hulking cruisers still soared towards the fleet, as if to smash through as Jafar had said.

"You were right," Jones said quietly.

"Yes, breach the defences and cause utter chaos. That is their job."

"And they're rolling right into our trap," Taylor said.

Two of the human ships were destroyed before their eyes. It brought a sober tone to them all, but only hardened their resolve to make the enemy pay dearly. As the Purge cruisers reached the fleet, another of the humans' ships was ripped apart by heavy pulses that tore it into four sections. The Neptune gave a vicious broadside from its guns as a cruiser passed. The salvo smashed the hull of the enemy ship and tore metal from its armour but did little to slow it down.

"Still sure we can breach that?" asked Jones.

"Yes," replied Jafar.

Glad someone is so optimistic, Mitch thought.

"Not long now till we kick their teeth in!" yelled Blinker.

Taylor smiled as the Private's brother shouted for him to be quiet. But in all honestly, he didn't mind it. They needed some rousing words and fighting spirit. He looked around to see that he was the only marine in their unit. Inter-Allied had become so closely knit since it all began that he had not given it a moment's thought.

"What are you thinking?" asked Jones.

"How I'm the only full blooded American here."

"You're the token yank," Jones replied with a smile.

Taylor could do nothing but laugh as he turned back to the viewing screen, checking the enemy's progress. They had to make light of the situation. It was the best way to calm their nerves at the realisation of what they were about to attempt. The first enemy cruiser struck a mine at the opening to the field. The device tore a chuck from the hull, but it continued on all the same until its power failed and it floated off as one more wreck in space.

"Got to be close now!"

"Wait for it, Eddie," replied Taylor.

He watched as the fighter wings from the Neptune soared through the enemy fleet, creating a wave of confusion and firing everything they had at the weapon ports of the cruisers. Taylor lifted his Mappad and allocated a ship to each platoon that was waiting before hitting the submit button.

"That's it, we're in place and good to go. Punch it!" he shouted.

Eddie was quick to respond. The engines were already running at minimal power and within a second were roaring. They lifted off from a rock that they and several other craft had been using for concealment. With full power down, they were rushing towards the lead enemy vessel at an immense pace. Eddie only let off the power at the last second, giving it full reverse thrust. They hit the hull of the cruiser hard, rocking all aboard, but they knew the impact would not have been felt inside the massive armoured beast.

Jones and his team got to work immediately. They opened the hatches and set the charges. Taylor was still doubtful they'd get through the thick skinned hull, but he was glad to have made it there alive, as they all were. There was a dull thud as the magnetic shaped charges were thrown against the hull of the enemy ship.

"Fire in the hole!"

They turned away as the button was pressed, and a sharp but short explosion erupted. It sounded more like a shotgun going off. Taylor turned in amazement to see a clean hole in the hull. They had gone through the inch thick blast doors that protected the windows to a cabin at the outer skin of the cruiser, as Jafar had said.

"We're in business!" Jones called out.

"Go!"

Jones was the first through the breach, and Taylor followed him. They had their weapons at the ready and shields held out to take an impact, but the room was peaceful. It reminded Taylor of the quarters he had occupied while on the Deveron. Some kind of workstation lay in the middle of the room, and an archway led to what appeared to be a bedroom. The layout was not unfamiliar, only the decor. A rack of what appeared to be either relics or trophies lay on a wall as prized possessions. Aside from a few weapons, Taylor did not recognise any of the items. Several appeared to be rifles and close quarter weapons, not of Mech origin, but he had little time to study them.

"We won't have long. The hull breach alert will already have activated," Jafar said.

"Lead the way," replied Taylor.

He stayed close to his alien friend as they were led down a long corridor that obviously led deep into the underbelly of the ship.

"Jesus, no wonder our guns can barely touch these things. The depth of this armour is like nothing we have ever seen," said Jones.

They finally reached a set of secure blast doors.

"Get these open," ordered Taylor.

Before the troops could act upon the order, several lights flashed and the doors before them prized open. Four Mechs stood in front of them with their weapons held low and unprepared. The eight members of the platoon at the front opened fire with vicious effect. The creatures were dead before they had known what hit them.

"They really underestimated us, didn't they?"

"This is the last thing they could have expected from us, Colonel," replied Jafar, as he stepped through the dead. "We're not far now."

They reached a four-way junction and stopped for a moment.

"The bridge is just up ahead."

Taylor turned back to the platoon.

"One section each way, as we planned it. Go."

He leapt forward with Jafar and Jones. This made Jones' section the strongest, but they were also heading for the main entrance. The corridor had only small strengthening girders each side, providing little cover. They were glad of the shields, or they'd be badly exposed. Taylor caught a glimmer of movement up ahead and realised it was the shape of two enemy soldiers guarding the doorway. They were raising their weapons as they too realised the threat.

"Fire!" he shouted.

Taylor didn't know if any of the others had spotted the creatures or not, but he knew the command would tell them everything they needed to know. There were thirty metres of open corridor between them and the enemy, but they did not slow their advance.

Holding their shields as barriers, they advanced with guns blazing. Taylor felt the heat of a pulse smash over his shield. The impact jolted his arm and reminded him of the pain from the shot that had blasted through when they had been boarded. It was also a pleasant reminder of how they were returning the favour.

A dozen or more shots pierced each of the Mechs' armour as they continued to cover the ground at almost a sprinting pace. Jafar got ahead of them and reached the doors first. He smashed his fist into the entry button, and the doors slid open. They were greeted by half a dozen of the enemy, waiting with their weapons at the ready. Three wore Mech armour that they were familiar with, but the others wore no armour at all, only their skin fitting body suits.

Pulses smashed into their shields, and the platoon split across the corridor, trying to hide from the volley of rounds coming through the open doorway. Taylor saw Blinker lifting a grenade from his webbing.

"No! We need the controls intact!"

It was too late, the grenade was launched through the air, and they couldn't risk trying to stop it. The explosion sent vibrations through the deck, and Taylor could only pray their plan had not failed at the pivotal point. Never before had he been so relieved that the enemy weapons continued to fire. The grenade must have bounced to the edge of the room.

"Wait for it! Wait!"

A few seconds later, another blast rang out from inside the bridge and another soon after that.

"Now!"

Taylor took the bend first and charged through the doorway, almost falling over the dead Mech on the deck. A single pulse rushed past his head, but the other targets were already occupied by the breaches in their bridge either side from the other sections. He let go of his rifle, allowing it to drop to his side, drawing out his Assegai as he continued his rush towards them.

The Colonel hit the first creature at full speed with his shield and sent it tumbling to the floor. He jumped onto the stunned alien, thrusting the weapon into its throat before it could recover. The lack of armour made it all the easier for the Assegai to pierce the skin.

A few cries and shots rang out around him. By the time

Taylor had pulled the weapon from his bloody victim, the bridge had been seized. He got to his feet and looked around in shock that it had gone so smoothly.

"You weren't wrong, Jafar."

The alien merely nodded as if surprised there was any other possibility.

"Jones, have a section set up defences here. Have the other two sweep and clear the ship."

As the Captain rushed off, the nuclear weapon was carted in and dumped at the very centre of the bridge among the enemy dead. Jafar pulled out the control module he had organised, twisted the power activator, and placed it onto a table beside one of the main consoles.

"How do you know how to do this?"

"High-ranking officers and Lords have wireless override keys which allow them to control a ship once on the bridge."

"But you are neither," replied Taylor.

"No, but information is power."

"Ain't that the truth?"

"Armed and ready to go, Sir."

"All right, good work."

He lifted his comms device up.

"This is Taylor. You have five minutes to complete your sweep."

"And us?" asked Jones.

"We stay with the nuke until everyone else is clear. It's

got an anti-tamper device, just in case we missed anyone on the sweep. Once we have left it, I want to be getting as far away as possible."

He sat back against the nearest console with a sigh.

"What is it?" asked Jones.

"Even if this works. If we somehow destroy or disable the Planet Killer and this Purge fleet all in one, we still have a long way to go."

"Yep, but that's not news to any of us, is it?"

Jones lay up opposite the Colonel with his rifle resting across his knees.

"You know when I was held by those bastards back so long ago, it was the hope of days like this which kept me going. Days when we would get to stick it to them."

He slapped his hand down on the nuclear weapon.

"Ramming a nuke down the bastards throats, that's just the ticket. They took almost everything from me. Not only that, they have taken Chandra as well. Until I find who was responsible for her death, I lay blame on their entire fucking race. Gone are the days when we run in fear and fight to their schedule. Today's the day we show them who's running this war."

Taylor nodded in agreement. He thought of Chandra.

I know she'd be gleefully smiling at the outcome we're heading for.

"Times up, everyone out now."

"You're right. I am gonna find out what happened to the Colonel before this war is over, and I will not rest until

I do. Leaving her out there is the biggest regret of my life."

"And yet you know all we could have done was followed her to her death."

He nodded.

"Yes," he whispered in return.

"Then let's honour her memory by blowing these bastards back to the hell they came from."

Jones turned to see Jafar had unintentionally heard everything from where he stood.

"You know what I said about those bastards doesn't extend to you? You are not one of them any longer."

"No, and I too lost that day. Tsengal was killed along with the Colonel, and I have no doubt he was with her at the end."

"All right, we'll have plenty of time to reflect when this is over. Or we'll all be dead and it won't matter," replied Taylor. "Let's move!"

CHAPTER FOUR

"Colonel Taylor, report immediately to the bridge."

He had been aboard the Neptune just two seconds. Enough to hear the cries and cheering of success as the troops of the 2nd Inter-Allied poured onto the docking bay decks following their successful mission. He wasn't going to leave until he'd checked his own people. He stepped into the centre of the deck where he could easily be seen and the officers find him. They all approached for a quick debrief.

"Well done to all of you, I want updates on your Companies...Jones?"

"One dead, four wounded."

"Grey?"

"Three dead, two wounded, Sir."

Jackson?"

"Three dead, none wounded."

"Ota?"

"We weren't needed in the end, Sir."

"All right, that's about the best we could have hoped for."

"One of my ships was hit and disabled on the way in, and I had to deploy my last platoon in their place. They have reported no wounded and crews are out recovering them now," Grey added.

"Good, get the wounded to medical. Re-equip and be ready for whatever comes at us next. Ota, I want your Company stationed here ready for rapid response via the Stallions. The rest of you know your grid sectors. Get to your posts and be ready for any possible breach in the hull. Well done, all of you."

He turned and strode off as ordered towards the bridge. Jafar was the only one who followed him. The alien would rarely ever leave his side, and it gave him a sense of security to know he had the strongest fighter in the fleet at his side at all times. He reached the bridge to find there was little sign of celebration amongst the crew.

"Colonel Taylor!" called Bailey.

She beckoned him over to the operations table where she was looking over the current enemy positions.

"Good work out their, Colonel. Be sure to pass on my congratulations to your people once this is all over. Of the Purge fleet, we destroyed two of the cruisers outright during the battle. Another two are disabled and one triggered one of the nukes not long after you departed. That leaves seven at our disposal loaded and ready to use. They have presently been set to continue their course to Earth in order to conceal our intentions. As far as the enemy is concerned, those still moving are still fighting with them."

"Then it worked," Taylor replied with relief.

"So far, yes. We are pulling back to the main fleet who will disperse and appear as if scattered from the Purge. We need them to bring this so called Planet Killer into the hornets' nest."

Taylor smiled. *Damn right, and ram it down the bastard's throat.*

"Have we had any sightings of the Planet Killer yet?"

"Ours scouts have confirmed it, yes. At their present speed, we'll have visual contact within the next ten minutes. I sure hope this thing needs to get as close as you say it does."

Taylor turned to Jafar for confirmation. He merely nodded in agreement in the calm fashion he always did.

"If it didn't, they would surely have come to a halt by now. No, they're coming for us."

"Now we just wait, and hope our guns are bigger than theirs. That our fleet is bigger than theirs, and our luck is better than theirs," whispered the Admiral.

"We can't have fought this hard for this long to have it all end now, can we?" Taylor asked.

It was a rhetorical question, and Bailey seemed to agree. "We've got incoming!"

They turned their attention back to the operations table to see pulses approaching.

"Evidently, their big guns are still bigger than ours," stated Taylor.

"Deploy counter measures!"

At the distance they were at, it still took time for the pulses to reach them, a fortunate thing indeed, considering the size of the shots. Cannons aboard the Neptune fired counter shots at the huge pulses and smashed them into thousands of particles well before they reached them.

"Much closer and we won't have that luxury," Bailey said.

"Targets will be in range in thirty seconds!"

"Prepare all weapons. I want to give them everything we've got from the get-go," she replied.

They could see the fighter wings advance from the human fleet. The Planet Killer was visible now, but they had been well prepared for it. To most who had fought the enemy in the first invasion of Earth, it looked little different to what they called Tartaros.

"Looks like they haven't got a whole load of ships covering that monster. You were right," Taylor said to Jafar.

"I doubt they think it's in any danger, not yet anyway," replied Bailey.

"In the Krycenaean history, the Gezgen K'til has been unstoppable. It is one of the things maintaining Demiran's power, for many of the other Lords fear its wrath, should he turn on them and try to expand his influence. Even the great Erdogan is wary of crossing Demiran for the power it holds."

"They really have pulled out the big guns," Taylor added.

"Yes, and played all their cards. If we can defeat this thing they all fear so much, we may well yet prove they can never win."

That was a positivity Taylor rarely heard. He liked this Admiral more every minute he served alongside her. Her confidence and composure reminded him a little of Chandra and that brought a smile to his face.

Almost there, he thought.

A single pulse flew past their display monitor and burrowed into the hull of the Neptune, but the dreadnought of a ship almost brushed it off entirely.

"In range in five, four, three, two."

"Fire," Bailey replied quickly.

The bridge lit up as the railguns and missile bays fired as one. The escort ships around the K'til took a battering from the human fleet, and as they closed the Earth planetary defence grid joining the fight. Taylor watched in awe as the battle unfolded before his eyes. From what they could see, it was just hulking ships slugging it out, but he also knew how many hundreds or thousands of lives were ended as each ship was blasted into space debris.

"Itching to get into combat, Colonel?" Bailey asked. Taylor stood mesmerised.

"It's strange to sit back and watch a battle be fought before your eyes. Never have I felt so redundant. Never have I seen death on the battlefield in such vast numbers. Some of those ships being vaporised have more men and women than my entire Battalion."

"Not a pretty sight, is it?"

"How much longer until we send the Purge fleet in?" he asked.

"Not long now, but we need to get as many of those escort ships out of the way as possible to give us the best chance of getting the nukes in. I just hope it's enough. Just look at the size of thing."

"Can't we just hit it with nukes from here?"

"We tried that last time around. Their weapon intercept defences took out everything we threw at them. Only way to get close is with something severely armoured."

"Then pray this works."

Taylor stepped forward and opened a channel to Huber.

"This is about the best opportunity I think we're gonna get, Sir."

"Agreed. Have your man activate the signal."

Taylor turned and nodded to Jafar who knew exactly what to do. He lifted a device he had kept close since they left the enemy vessels and punched in a few buttons.

"That it?"

He nodded in acknowledgement. Bailey placed her hand on the ops table and panned over to where the Purge ships had laid in wait beyond the human fleet.

"They're powering up. This is it."

The battle continued to rage all around them, but Bailey and Taylor were fixated on the Purge ships on their viewing screens. They knew it was their best and probably only chance of stopping the Planet Killer.

"Has anyone ever tried to destroy this thing before?"

"Yes, Admiral. They failed," he replied sternly.

"I guess they didn't have inside knowledge like we do."

Jafar remained silent.

"How long until they reach their target?"

"Approximately two minutes, Ma'am."

"The game must be up by now that we have control over them. Direct all fire to supporting their approach, and notify the rest of our battle group to do the same."

"Looks like Huber has already had the main fleet doing that," said Taylor.

They looked out to see a brutal bombardment hitting everything between them and the massive Planet Killer. The seven Purge cruisers soared in between Bailey's battle group and the main fleet with their engines at full. There was no hiding it anymore. Within seconds of them passing, a volley of pulses smashed into the first vessel, ripping it apart. Several of the bridge crew gasped at the brutal salvo that continued onto the second ship but didn't manage to slow it any.

"Come on, come," whispered Taylor.

He could see Bailey wanted to give them more, but the Neptune was already firing with everything she had. Now they could only watch and pray. The distance was closing rapidly between the Purge ships and the K'til. The second ship began to spit sparks until a final burst blew it apart.

"Shit," Taylor murmured.

He doubted for a minute that any would get through,slumping his head down as he leaned against the table.

"It's not over yet," replied Bailey.

He hadn't realised he had spoken so loudly for others to hear. He knew he had a responsibility to maintain confidence in their endeavour. As he lifted his head, a great light grew in size and brightness on the edge of the K'til hull. They all stared in surprise and amazement until they realised what it was. A weapon Taylor had witnessed during their Tau Ceti expedition. It was a devastating ship killer. The light suddenly rushed from the ship towards the Purge fleet and struck one across its prow. The ship shattered into thousands of parts in seconds, and what was left was unidentifiable as anything but space debris.

They're not gonna make it, Taylor thought.

The weapon powered up once again and obliterated

another of the cruisers.

"Come on," said Bailey.

Taylor looked up at the last minute when he knew the monstrous weapon could not fire again before the distance was closed. The entire bridge crew watching silently as the last three Purge cruisers still moving plunged into the K'til. They smashed through the outer hull with little resistance at all. They punctured deep within and continued until they were no longer visible.

Sighs of reliefs came from all the crew, but all was not over. Bailey spun around to look directly into Jafar's eyes.

"Do it!"

He did not hesitate, and Taylor was frozen solid watching the display screen. Ripples ran through the front of the K'til until cracks appeared and the blast burst out of the structure, tearing frigate size pieces from the outer skin. Explosions erupted through the ship, and the massive pulse cannon was ripped apart.

"Yes!" yelled Bailey.

Cheers echoed around the bridge as the crew leapt up from their seats in celebration. She turned to Jafar.

"Thank you, you've done us a damn good turn."

He nodded in agreement in his typically calm character. Bailey turned back to the ops table where Taylor had not moved, and her smile was quickly erased.

"They're still coming at us," he whispered.

"Their defence grid must be down with all that damage.

Launch nukes into that breach, now!"

The gunnery officer stood speechless with his mouth open.

"Fire the damn nukes now!"

"Admiral!" Taylor shouted.

She spun around to see a large metallic glowing object soar towards the fleet, but it did not appear to be targeting any ship in particular. Jafar recognised it immediately, but he did not have any time to warn them, not that it would have helped. They all stared as boosters came on to draw it to a standstill, and then it erupted with a shockwave. Just three seconds later the bridge went dark. All lights, power, and displays shut off.

"What the hell just happened?" Bailey cried out.

Taylor felt the weight of his Reitech suit almost drag him to the ground as its power source had also cut out, and he felt three times heavier than a second ago. He reached for the catches to release the suit from his body, and it hit the deck with a loud crash.

"That was an EMP!" he answered.

For a few moments there was complete blackness. Deep in the core of the hull of the Neptune they were a long way from any windows that would bring in any light. Even if they were closer to the outer skin, the blast shields were up. The entire ship was not in blackout; thirty seconds later, lights flickered across the bridge and emergency lighting powered up. It was a muted red ambient lighting, but it was enough to get by.

"That's the reserve power source kicking in. It's shielded against EMPs but will only power basic life support. Enough for us to get working," the Admiral explained.

Taylor turned to Jafar for answers and didn't even have to ask.

"This is an act of desperation. The EMP will have disabled the vessels of both sides. Demiran must have seen the end was close for the Gezgen K'til. He is scared."

"That's all very well, but it leaves us hanging," replied the Admiral.

"How far will this have spread?"

"Only those ships on the very fringe of this fight would have escaped it."

"You're telling me there are hundreds of ships floating in space without power, just like us?" she asked.

"Yes. The EMP cannot be directed. Like you, the Krycenaeans' vessels have only limited shielding, as it is impractical to have it all encompassing. However, they are better prepared for this."

"You're saying they'll get active before us?"

"Almost certainly."

"Christ, if they can get that monster going before our ships recover, they can fire on Earth without anyone to stop them," she replied.

"Is there no one left to continue the fight?" Taylor asked.

She looked up into his eyes with fear and shook her head.

"We committed everything we had to this, how could we not? The greatest threat the World has ever known?"

"So let me get this straight. Both fleets are floating about without power. You reckon they'll fix the Planet Killer before we can get any ships online, and that'll be the end?" he asked of Jafar.

The alien nodded in agreement.

"Well, fuck that. We didn't get through years of this shit to sit here and watch it all end."

"There's nothing else to do. Our crews will already have started work. We can only hope they get us operational before we're blasted by their weapons."

"And what would we go home to? No way. I won't accept it."

He lifted up his comms unit.

"Lieutenant Rains to the bridge..."

He realised the comms units were down as well. It would be weeks of repair work until everything was restored.

"How long do we have till the Planet Killer is operational?"

"Two hours, maybe."

"Allright. Maybe we can't get the Neptune up and running in that time, but we can surely get marines into action before then."

"What are you thinking?" asked Bailey.

"I'm thinking we'll hand deliver those nukes gift wrapped, " he replied confidently.

"Anything you need, Colonel. The only thing that matters anymore is destroying that ship. It doesn't matter what it costs. Take any resources you need. Your mission must come before the repair of this ship. Within the emergency shielded core, you will find a reserve of armour and weapons, along with a few other core components. You have the full resources of this crew at your disposal. I don't care how you do it, or at what cost, just get it done!"

Taylor nodded in acceptance of the mission. He knew it was unlikely anyone else in the fleet would have the information, ability, or initiative to act against the K'til. The fate of Earth now lay in his hands. He gestured for Jafar to follow him, grabbing his Reitech rifle from the deck. Without the support of his exo-skeleton, it weighed a tonne. They rushed from the bridge at a quick pace. Taylor felt more vulnerable than ever. He had no armour, no communications, no power, and a rifle he could barely carry.

Two minutes into their run they bumped into Jones and one of his platoons. They'd setup in defensive positions around an air lock. Taylor could see the Captain was anticipating a breach at any moment. They too had stripped off their armour and suits that had become dead weights. Jones arose from cover as he saw them approach. He looked flabbergasted.

"EMP? What the hell's going on?"

"Both fleets are out. I don't have time to get into the details. A breach isn't our concern, right now. We're heading for the docking bays. Join us, and I'll fill you in on the way."

"Doesn't sound good. Follow the Colonel!" he ordered.

"I'd love to say it's the same shit, different day, but this time, it's a whole lot worse."

It took them just a few minutes to reach the bay where they had left Ota's Company. Only she and one platoon now remained.

"Sir, we didn't know what the hell was going on. I have dispatched units to defend the nearest ports."

He acknowledged her as he rushed past without a word to get to Rains. He was sanding on top of a crate with his head and torso up inside the engine bay of his Stallion.

"Eddie, tell me you can get this bird going!"

"Not without the parts, Colonel. The CPU is fried, and a few other components that she won't run without."

"I might be able to get what you need from the emergency stores," he replied.

"That could work. We still have some major issues though. She's gonna need more than a few bits."

He reached forward and grabbed the pilot's arm, hauling him down.

"I need you flying in the next thirty minutes, or Earth will be destroyed. Is that enough motivation?"

He looked down into Taylor's eyes for a second and saw the seriousness in his face.

"Well, holy shit, you aren't joking."

He jumped down to the deck, and his tone had changed completely.

"Get me to the parts!"

He looked over to his co-pilot and the Engineering Chief who had been helping him, pointing for them to follow him.

"Jones, you and your platoon with me, come on!" yelled Taylor.

They rushed towards the nearest corridor, and Taylor lifted his Mappad to check the location of the emergency stores.

"God damn it."

It was another piece of technology disabled by the blast. He turned back to the Chief, knowing he knew the ship better than anyone.

"The emergency storeroom, take us to it."

Without a word, the Chief rushed forward to lead the way. He too had heard Taylor's grim insight into their future, should they fail in their task. Eddie was running alongside the Colonel and still in shock at what was being proposed.

"No bullshit about this, we get flying or it's all over?"

"That's right."

"So you're pinning the entire survival of the World on

our ability to bodge an EMP hit Stallion which will get you what, a one-way ticket riding nukes into the biggest mother fucking ship I have ever seen?"

"That's about the sum of it, yeah."

"Well I hate to say it, Colonel, I might be a mechanical wizard, but I ain't no miracle worker."

"Today you are."

"This is it!" called the Chief.

He punched in the access codes, and thankfully the huge shielded blast doors slid open. The room was the size of a tennis court and a couple of metres high.

"This is everything we have that'll still work after an EMP."

Jones rushed inside and hauled the Chief alongside him.

"Please be in here, please be in here," whispered Eddie.

Taylor could see a rack of Reitech equipment.

"That's at least something. Must be enough to kit out all of us here. Gear 'em up, Captain," he ordered Jones.

"You heard the man!"

They quickly strapped themselves into the suits, a drill which they had become more than used to doing in quick time. As Taylor secured the last clips onto his arms, Eddie approached with a large trolley stacked with component parts.

"We got some of what we need. Most of this stuff is last gen, and we'll only get the bare bones up and running.

Maybe the engines and manual controls, no weapons, life support, grav, scanners, comms, nothing."

"Just get her flying, that's all we need!"

He continued on to the corridor.

"Chief, I'll need you and a dozen of your best to have a hope in hell of getting this done!"

"Anything you need," he replied, and they rushed away with the cart.

"What's the play here?" asked Jones.

"Exactly what it looks like. We're hand delivering a few nukes."

"Doesn't sound like the best plan in the world. They must have thousands of Mechs aboard that thing, maybe even tens of thousands."

"Yep, and we have just one long shot of making this work. If you can think of something better, I'm all ears. Otherwise, prepare for a ride into hell."

He turned back to address Jones' platoon.

"By now, you probably all have idea of what we're about to do. I am sorry to say you have ended up on this mission through the shear bad luck of being in the wrong place at the wrong time. I needed assistance, and you were the first I reached. However, we have been together since the very beginning, and there's nobody I'd rather trust to undertake this mission. I know you want to live, and do not believe for a moment that I have a death wish. But this mission is more important than any of our lives. If we have to give up a few dozen to save a few billion, so be it. But let's not give those lives willingly."

It was a lot to take in for a group of veteran soldiers who had so recently been preparing to fight en masse on their own ground with all the support of the Battalion and Navy crews.

"Let's be clear here. If there is any chance we can make it out alive, then we will, but only once our mission is complete. Grab you gear and another half a dozen sets,and let's haul ass back to Rains."

When they were on the move in the corridor, Jones finally spoke again.

"You promise me something, Mitch."

"Anything."

"Dying fighting these bastards is not something I fear, but being taken alive by them again is. You promise me you won't let that happen. Whatever happens over there, you promise me that!"

It was a sombre thought, but Taylor fully understood where he was coming from, and it was not the first time Jones had asked it.

"If it ever came to it, you have my word, but it won't. We have debts to pay, and there won't be any dying until those scores are settled."

Jones nodded in acknowledgement. That was something he certainly agreed with.

They arrived back at the docking bay to find twenty

mechanics going at the Stallion like never before. Sparks were flying as components were cut and welded. Rains' head was buried in the access hatch where they had first found him when it had all begun.

"Where are we up to, Rains?" Taylor asked.

He finished tightening something down before ducking back down to see the Colonel.

"It ain't pretty, but we have a chance of making this work."

Taylor breathed out a sigh of relief.

"And how long will this masterpiece take?"

"In ten minutes she'll either run, or it's all over."

"Then get on it and be sure it works," Taylor snapped back.

Rains held up his hands as if to complain that he was already being distracted. Taylor turned to see the platoon all stood there, watching the work. It was hard to tell if they were keen for it to be successful or not.

"I want two full suits prepared for the pilots. They'll need them as much as us, including weapons."

As he was speaking, Silva pushed through the ranks to reach the Colonel.

"Sir, permission to join you."

"We have limited space here, Sergeant Major, if we get off the deck at all."

"Sir, you need all the help you can get. You have a few spare sets of gear, and I don't see many volunteers taking them up."

Taylor sighed and shrugged his shoulders.

We're already putting two key officers of the unit in danger, but it doesn't seem to matter anymore.

"What the hell, I haven't got the will to argue anymore. Just do me one thing, get word to Parker's section that they are to stay put. I don't want her knowing about this mission. You do that,and you get a seat on this ride."

"Aye, aye, Sir."

Silva seemed excited by the news, which astonished Taylor.

He must be mad. Still, I'm glad to have the Sergeant Major by my side.

"So this is it, thirty-three against the World?" asked Jones.

"Plus Eddie and his co-pilot,Perez, and a handful of nukes."

"Sounds like an interesting recipe."

Taylor looked down the docking bay and could see Kato working on one of the other Stallions with a repair crew, but they weren't getting anywhere near the attention and work put in that Rains was. He could see it would be some time before the other craft were up and running.

The next ten minutes seemed more like an hour as the platoon lay about on the nearest boxes watching Eddie and the others slave away as quickly as they could. Jafar sat one side of Taylor and Jones the other.

"Assuming we get inside this thing, what then?" asked Jones.

Taylor turned and looked to Jafar for answers.

"If they launched an EMP, then the situation must have been desperate. There must be a hull breach so severe that much more damage, and the K'til would be inoperable. The power source and weapon itself is at the very core of the ship. If we want to guarantee success, then we must get your nuclear weapons as deep into the vessel as possible."

"How far are we talking?" asked Jones.

"At least a kilometre in."

"Christ!"

"But we have already done a tonne of damage, so we should be able to fly a good way inside the structure," replied Taylor.

"The crews will still be in chaos trying to recover and repair the ship. Their communications will be out of service just as ours, but it will not be long until they recover."

Engines pulsated before them as Rains' Stallion fired up. Cheers rang out from the crews all around, but not from Jones' platoon. All Rains' success meant to them in that moment was that they would have to enter the jaws of death. Rains' voice rang out as he shouted for Perez to test the controls before he finally jumped down to address the Colonel.

"We have power and basic controls, but that's it."

"That's all we need."

Eddie wiped the sweat from his brow, which was as much from working as it was the stress he had been placed under.

"Suit up."

Rains turned and gestured for Perez to get back to the deck and do likewise.

"Make way!" a voice yelled.

Taylor already recognised it as Admiral Bailey.

"Attention on deck!"

"As you were!" she hollered back.

She strolled out onto the docking bay deck, with twenty crew in tow. At the head of the column, they wheeled in three nuclear weapons."

"This is the entire compliment for the Neptune, so use them well."

I hope it'll be enough. It was all Taylor could think.

She stepped in close so she could address him privately.

"You really think this can work?" she asked him.

"In all the crazy suicidal plans I have heard and participated in, this has to be the most ridiculous, but we haven't failed or died yet."

"I guess that's hopeless optimism."

"Not hopeless. This has to work, and I'll give it everything to make it happen."

"I wish there was more we could do. It's crazy that with all these ships and all this man power, it's going to come down to what, thirty marines?"

Jones could just hear what she was saying from his position behind Taylor and coughed deliberately at hearing his troops being called marines.

"Captain Jones, isn't it?" she asked.

"Yes, Ma'am."

She looked down at his uniform to see he still wore the Parachute Regiment patches and British Union Flag adorning his sleeves. It was clear the insignia was much older and more fatigued than the rest of his attire, and she could tell it had been carried over to every uniform he had worn since the fighting began."

"No, not marines. Does it matter anymore, Navy, Marines, Army, Paras? We're all in the same shit and fighting the same battle. On behalf of the Navy, I extend my gratitude for the sacrifices that you are about to make. Make it home or not, it will never be forgotten."

"Unless we fail, and there will be no one left to remember it," Jones jested.

Bailey could not refrain from smiling. It pleased her to see their spirits were high. Taylor looked around to see Rains and Perez were kitted up and ready to move. They were waiting at the door to their Stallion and overseeing the loading of the nukes.

"Ma'am, we have precious little time."

"Good luck," she said, as she reached out to shake Taylor's hand.

He looked around to the crew who were with her and mechanics to their sides. A sombre tone filled the room. Gone was the eager enthusiasm and momentum to fix the Stallion. The celebrations had already died down as they realised the real trial was about to begin.

"We're doing everything we can do get operational again. If we can assist before this is over, we will," Bailey added.

"Load up! Let's move!"

The platoon rushed to the door, but Taylor stopped as he heard his name screamed from down the corridor Bailey had so recently travelled. Personnel scattered as someone pushed their way through to reach him. His name was screamed once again, and he recognised it instantly. It was Parker. Before she was visible, he turned to Silva with a scornful look.

"I told you to make sure she didn't find out."

"And I did, but you know what she's like."

He shook his head, but he knew the Sergeant Major was right.

Eli broke through the ground and leapt onto him in front of the Admiral without a care for her presence. First she hugged him and then recoiled to confront him.

"What the hell are you doing?" she asked.

"Our jobs, and don't go thinking you're going to join us."

"It's suicide, Mitch!"

"Colonel!" Eddie called.

He turned around to see the last of the platoon were getting through the door, and they were ready to go. He looked back to Eli whose eyes could not hide how distraught she felt.

"No, suicide is doing nothing. We have to act and do it now. I'm sorry, but I can't waste another moment."

"No! Mitch!"

He turned and left. She tried to follow, but the Admiral's guards grabbed hold of her and held her back. She began to weep, but she quickly wiped the tears from her face and shrugged off the guards. She turned to make one last appeal to the Admiral.

"Why him? Haven't we given enough? Haven't we sacrificed enough?"

"Taylor is Earth's best hope. Would you rather leave it to a lesser officer?"

She shook her head and knew it was the right, or at least the best course of action, but it didn't make it any easier to accept. The Admiral continued.

"The best thing we can do for him is get this ship operational and stay safe. We still don't know what's out there, and without our comms, we are in serious danger if we are breached. You have a position to guard. I suggest you get back to it, and make sure Taylor has something to come home to."

Her shoulders relaxed as she accepted the situation and

stood calmly to watch them leave.

"What chance do you think he has?" she asked Bailey.

The Admiral was accepting the Sergeant's over familiarity, as she knew it was a tough situation to digest.

"Of destroying the K'til or getting back alive?" she replied.

"I do not doubt he will succeed. Taylor is not one to fail. He wasn't born with the ability to fail. The only question is what is the cost of success?"

Bailey had no answer. She knew just as Parker did that Taylor would not hesitate to give up everything to get the job done.

"If anyone can make it back, Mitch can."

Taylor stepped aboard the Stallion and stopped in the doorway to look at her one last time. He then turned to step inside but stopped as he noticed a hastily applied lettering sprayed across the fuselage. It read 'Welcome to Earth you bastards'. It brought a smile to his face, and he knew that only Eddie could have done it. Mitch hit the door close switch and it did nothing. He smiled before cursing.

"Fuck this is gonna be a real barrel of laughs."

He turned around and grabbed the door of the ramp, hauling it shut by hand before clamping the mechanism shut.

"Back to basics, ey Colonel?" asked Blinker.

"Be thankful we have our personal gear. Think back to

before the days of Reitech, and you'll appreciate what we do have."

"Yeah, I will when we're blasting back off that big mother fucking ship," he replied with a smirk.

Taylor couldn't doubt he felt any different. He knew the mission had to be done, and he knew he needed to be the one to do it, but now it was finally going ahead he could feel the sickness in his stomach return. The sickness that always came before such a vital mission. The engines roared, and they lifted off from the deck, soaring out towards the exit.

"This isn't the first time Earth has faced an apocalyptic weapon, or the first time I have led the operation to destroy it. We've done it before, and we'll do it again. Let's remind these bastards what happens when you mess with our planet!"

Cheers rang out. It was the first time he had gone into an operation with an almost entirely British force, but there seemed little difference between any of the personnel of Inter-Allied any longer. Silva had a broad grin on his face, the only one of them who did.

"What are you so pleased about?" asked Taylor.

"Honestly, it's hard to say. We're going all in here, no time to regret it any longer."

Taylor still didn't get it, but it was better than the sombre tone that they had left at the dock.

CHAPTER FIVE

Rains' Stallion soared out of the Neptune's docking doors just a few metres from the crew who had to open the doors manually. The whole operation felt like a hash job, but it was the best they could muster. Taylor made his way to the cockpit through the cramped cabin. He wished he could have taken the whole Battalion, but with the nukes loaded as well, there was no space left.

"Look at it," said Eddie. "They may have launched that EMP in desperation, but we weren't doing a whole lot better."

Mitch reached the pilot and could now see what he meant. The wreckage of many ships from both sides floated through space, and Eddie had to navigate his way carefully through the debris. Fortunately, it covered their approach to the K'til. It was hard to tell if some ships were still crewed by survivors or not, as both fleets were without power.

"You better hope they still have no power, or this is gonna be one short mission."

"If they knew we were coming, you'd not even have got those words off, Eddie."

"Hope so."

It took just a few minutes for them to reach the Gezgen K'til. Rains cut the engines a long way out, letting them drift and appear as incapacitated as the rest. In the distance, a few ships and fighters still slugged it out on the very edge of the battle beyond the range of the EMP. The K'til was badly damaged from the impact and looked almost as if a huge bite had been taken from it, but one that didn't penetrate more than ten percent into the diameter of the hulking beast.

"I thought sure we'd have done more damage than that, hoped at least," said Taylor.

Nobody responded, so he continued.

"If the Purge ships and their nukes couldn't finish this thing, how'd you know these three nukes will do it?"

"I don't," replied Jafar.

"Well that's bloody great," Jones said, smiling.

Taylor was starting to understand why Silva had been so jovial as they set off. Like Jones, he had reverted to light heartedness in order to save himself from the soul destroying fear any sane person would feel if confronted with their mission. Yet he was the only one who volunteered to go, and that pleased Taylor greatly. Several of them were looking to Jafar after his rather ambiguous and vague answer to the most important question of their lives. He could see they were awaiting an answer.

"Do you think I have ever destroyed something like the K'til before? Just because I have stepped foot aboard it, does not mean I can guarantee a way to destroy it."

"He's right," insisted Taylor. "This isn't just our best chance. It's our only chance."

"Pretty close now. I'm gonna have to use some power to slow us down, or we'll wipe out," said Eddie.

"Then we have to assume any enemy with visual contact will know immediately that something is going on," replied Taylor.

"I'll do my best, but someone's gonna see it."

They continued to drift into the hole that had been blasted in the great enemy ship. It was like travelling along a vast canyon but with twisted and wrecked metalwork all around. They were closing quickly now on the furthest point to where the damage penetrated into the K'til.

"What's that there?" Taylor asked Eddie.

There was a glimmer of movement up ahead and sparks of light on a large exposed room where one wall and the roof had been blasted away. The floors above and below were also exposed as if looking in at a cutaway diagram of the vessel.

"If I had to guess, I'd say a repair crew."

"All right, head right for 'em. Use as little power as you can."

"What have you got in mind?"

"If we put down anywhere round here, there's a good chance they'll see us anyway. I want to hit them first, and try and minimise any chance of them passing on our arrival."

"Okay, so how'd you want to play this?"

Put down just enough power to save any damage, and let us drift into the floor above them. Make it look like this is another wreck of space debris."

"Hell there's enough of it around. This might just work."

"When we hit the deck, you must both stick with us. Leave the doors to the Stallion open, and make it look like it really is an empty wreck. I don't want any Mechs stumbling upon two pilots waiting with the engines running."

"You really think we're gonna make it back off this thing?"

"Hell, yeah, I'm too young to die," Taylor replied lightly.

Rains could not help but laugh.

"Well, all right. I can bring our speed down with bow thrusters alone. That shouldn't draw any more attention than us barrelling in like a piece of junk."

Eddie turned off the last console lights. They were in complete blackout now as they floated into the mouth of the enemy vessel.

"You know if this thing hadn't come to destroy our planet, I might actually be genuinely impressed," whispered Eddie.

"Yeah, well save your genuinely impressed expression for when we blow it sky high," replied Taylor.

"So you expecting us to fight too?" asked Perez.

"If you have to, yes. Rains here proved himself more than capable last time the shit hit the fan and he was left with a gun in his hands. We're few, and they are many, so I need every fighter I can get."

"Been a long time since I had to shoot anything."

"Not for long it won't be, Eddie."

"This is it, no turning back now."

Taylor turned back to Jones' and his platoon and whispered.

"We're faking a crash landing and coming down right over what looks like a repair crew. I want us out the door and taking them down immediately."

He turned back just in time to see them pass over the enemy position and smash down onto the floor of the next level. They slid along the metal floor, causing sparks to spray up either side of them before grinding to a halt. It was just enough to make it look like their craft was a wreck, but controlled enough to cause no more than superficial damage.

"Let's go," whispered Taylor.

Jones was first to the door and heaved the large slider aside but forgot the lack of power. The ramp dropped like a brick and smashed down onto the floor. He cringed but relaxed as he realised it was probably no louder than the bull in a china shop landing that Eddie had just strived for. The platoon was frozen and waiting for a response to the noise, but it did not come. Jones turned, pointing for them to move. He was the first one down the ramp and rushed to the ragged edge of the floor that was exposed to space itself.

As they reached the edge, they ground to a halt and looked down realising the drop onto the other decks and space itself. The low gravity of the space before them would present no danger should they fall, but it did not stop Jones' from feeling unsettled. It was like looking over the edge of a skyscraper. Despite being a Parachute regiment officer, he had still never fully gotten over his discomfort with heights.

Taylor reached the edge beside him and looked down to see one of the Mech workers lifting a weapon to the slightly mesmerised Captain. Taylor quickly fired two carefully aimed shots, hitting the creature square in the chest. It wore an armoured suit that the Reitech rounds punctured through and exited out the other side of the alien's body. The creature fell back and floated off the ship into space. Any other time, Taylor would fear the body being discovered, but this day it would be just another corpse among the thousands of others in space.

Out of the corner of his eye, he noticed something move, but before he could respond, Jones' weapon fired, and two others joined him. Two more of the creatures were instantly killed without getting a shot off. Jafar reached them and looked at the repair work being undertaken.

"Those crews work in threes, so there should be no others in sight."

"Good, then let's move. You lead the way."

He turned to see the three nukes were already in tow. With the low gravity and power of the Reitech suits just two men could carry each. Jafar led the way forward, but Taylor turned back to Jones and could see he was every bit as concerned for the operation as he was.

"Only way is forward, old chap."

"Yeah, Jones, that's what I'm afraid of. Come on, let's see this through."

The two of them led the platoon on with Jafar on point. He led them back past Rains' Stallion and through the blast damaged room until they were into the core of the ship. On their route, they past several dead aliens, but there was little sign of any other movement.

"Where is everyone, Jafar?" whispered Taylor.

"There will be roving patrols, but the impact must have killed many. Most of those aboard will be busy fixing the breaches."

"So they're forming a perimeter all around this blast

site. How are we supposed to get in?" asked Jones.

"Through one of Demiran's many access tunnels. There are secret passageways throughout all of his personal ships that only he and his personal guard know how to recognise."

"Sounds like he doesn't have a whole lot of trust for his own people?" replied Jones.

"No, there are many who would not hesitate to kill the Lord if they were ever given the opportunity. Surely this is not an unfamiliar concept to humans?"

Taylor could not help but smile.

"It isn't those under my command I fear. It's those above it."

"Lions led by sheep," Jones added.

Jafar seemed confused by the expression, and it was clear he wasn't sure what either of the animals was.

"You can speak our language, but you don't know what a lion is?"

"Our translation chips allow us to converse, but for some things there are no translations. There are creatures on my homeworld which I could not begin to explain to you in any language you would understand."

"Fair enough," replied Jones.

"Come on, let's focus on the task at hand," said Taylor. How confident are you that our presence has gone unnoticed?"

"Absolute. They would be hunting us right now if they

knew we were aboard. The last thing Demiran would ever expect is for the humans to try and board the Gezgen K'til."

"Why?"

"Just look at it, Captain," replied Taylor.

"Yes, it has become the thing of nightmares. To go near it would be to invite death to all around you."

"Good to know, Jafar," said Jones.

Up ahead they could see an open doorway.

"Come."

They paced quickly but cautiously down the corridor to the broad doorway which was three metres wide by two high. One of the two doors look at if it had tried to shut but was jammed against the floor which had buckled up and blocked its path.

"They'll be along to fix this before long."

As soon as they had all got through, Jafar heard movement and signalled for them to shift over into the side of the corridor. Taylor ducked down into the alcove, realising how vulnerable he felt not having his shield. They had rushed so quickly into the mission, and they had to be as light and subtle as possible, that it would not have been practical to take them. But he sure wished for it now. Jafar leaned in close.

"Two sentries."

Taylor lifted his hand and signalled the news to the others as he drew his Assegai, lifting it for all to see. It was all the message they needed.

"Let's do this quietly."

Jafar's rifle was already slung down. He had known it was the way to do it.

I wonder if my alien friend has always been so adept at fighting in a dirty and clandestine way rather than the stand up fight the Mechs seem to use. He's so different from the regular alien soldiers that I have to assume he's been something special from the beginning.

The heavy footsteps grew nearer and stayed at a steady pace. The slow amble of a bored security detail sweeping large areas. It reminded him of some of the mindless duties he had been given as a young officer. He'd give anything to return to those long boring details. His pulse increased as the steps grew louder until finally a gun barrel swept into view. Jafar leapt into action and thrust his Assegai up under the arm of the first, driving it deep into the creature's torso for an instant kill.

The second creature was quick to respond by pivoting its weapon around to fire on Jafar, but with one quick kick he shoved it out the way. Before he could close the distance, the creature spasmed from an impact from behind. It tried to turn but was hit several more times and toppled down to the deck. Blinker stood over the vanquished body with thick blood pouring from the tip of his Assegai.

"They said never stab a man in the back, but not these things," he said with a smile.

Monty shook his head in despair.

"We're on the most important and suicidal mission of our lives, and you still find time to lark about," he whispered.

Taylor looked down at the body that had been hit by repeated thrusts through its backplate. He looked up to the cocky Private who still had a broad grin on his face.

"Should we hide the bodies?" Jones asked.

"No, there is no time," replied Jafar as he lifted his rifle back into his hands and continued on.

"You seem to know this ship well," Taylor said, joining him at the front.

"No, but all of Demiran's vessels were made in his shipyard and follow the same basic layout."

"Makes sense if he wanted to easily locate and use those secret access tunnels he has."

"Yes."

They continued on until they reached a broad door that was sealed shut.

"This is where they have sealed the ship from the damage. The only way in now is through Demiran's passageways."

Taylor lifted his arm, looking at the time with concern.

"You said we had maybe an hour to get this done. Forty-five minutes have already passed. This is getting a little close for comfort."

"The weapon takes three minutes to power up, and you will know when that starts."

"Three minutes? Let's hope we don't have to hear that sound."

"I have never heard it myself either. I only know of it from legend."

"All right, then let's get to this secret entrance and be on our way."

Jafar was looking up and around the walls, clearly searching for some unique signature only a select knew to look for. The lighting was barely enough to get by. Clearly the K'til had some basic power back. Helpful for getting their job done, but also disconcerting knowing what they were getting the power back online for.

"You still think Demiran is aboard?" asked Taylor.

"Yes, the K'til is only ever commanded by him. It would be an insult for anyone else to have had the honour of destroying a world with the K'til."

"Great, what I wouldn't give to get my hands on him."

Jafar turned to Taylor.

"I think your chance will come before long."

Jafar turned away and followed the wall, constantly looking up and down. Taylor wasn't sure whether he was following some hidden signs or completely lost, but he dare not ask. Eventually, he stopped, reaching the vent to what appeared to be a duct system. It was a metre square at most.

"Seriously? That's the 'secret access'?" asked Jones with scepticism.

Jafar pulled open the vent but did not climb in. Instead, he put his arm in, reaching up as far as he could. A second later, there was a hiss like gas escaping, and a door swung open a metre further along. Taylor breathed a sigh of relief. It was the first sign that the plan might actually work.

"Not that I doubted you, but holy shit! This is like some hidden King's corridor in an old castle," Jones grinned.

"Precisely. It is entirely mechanical and powered by compressed gas, allowing the doors to be activated even if the power is down. This will take us about thirty metres and far inside the perimeter they have set."

Taylor stepped cautiously towards the doors, considering the fact they were committing everything they had into one corridor with only one way in and one way out.

This could be our valley of death, he thought.

"Are you positive nobody will know we are here?" he asked.

"Demiran will not think for a minute this access has been compromised. Last he saw I was loyal to him. He must think me dead, if he has given any thought at all to Tsengal and me."

"You saved his life when we first met, did you not?"

"Yes, but that will mean little to him. As far as Demiran is concerned, every Krycenaean owes their life to him."

"Nice," Taylor replied, gesturing for Jafar to lead the way. Jones stayed at the back to see the door shut after they were all inside. They stepped quietly along the passageway, not knowing what lay either side of them through the thick walls. They reached the far end without incident, but then came the time to enter into an unknown area. Taylor had his rifle at the shoulder, and Jafar reached for the door, counting down with his finger as he had been trained to do.

The door swung open, and Taylor stepped out quickly. He expected to have to fight his way out of the doorway, but there was nothing. Not a single sign of life. He signalled for the others to join him.

"How much further do we need to go?"

"Just another hundred metres should do it."

"Should?"

Jafar nodded.

They continued on down a broad corridor with four metre high ceilings. Tracks lay along the floor that looked as if they were some kind of tramline for moving heavy goods. They covered half the distance they needed when they reached a bend. Time was short, so they blundered on without checking blind corners. As they took the bend, shock nearly stopped Taylor's heart, and they came to a halt. A dozen Mechs were marching towards them. Their weapons were lowered, and it was clear they were as surprised as each other. Neither moved for a few seconds.

Jones was the first to fire, and it was the signal for the others to join him. Outnumbered three to one, the Mechs didn't stand a chance and only managed to fire off a few pulses before they all lay dead from the devastating volley. Taylor looked back, and to his amazement and delight, they had not taken a single casualty.

"That was as much luck as anything."

None of them were in any doubt. They were just glad to be alive.

"This is the entrance to one of the main crossroads of the tunnel system. Your nuclear weapons will yield maximum effect here."

"I can't believe we're gonna get away with planting these. How are they not on to us yet?" asked Jones.

"They will be," replied Jafar. "That gun battle will not have gone unnoticed. We have to hurry."

They got to a jogging pace. The corridor opened out as Jafar said into a huge five way crossroads with a domed roof. It was completely empty, but Taylor noticed the tramlines from every corridor converged at centre.

"Why is there no one here?"

"This is a main storage facility. Everything stored here will have been loaded ready for the weapon."

"What does it fire, this thing?" asked Jones.

"I have no idea. That is a secret Demiran and his ancestors have kept well guarded. That secret maintains the power they have."

"Then it will die with him," replied Taylor.

"We can only hope," Jones added.

The nukes were carried into the crossroads area. Jafar

was pacing around the huge room until he found what he was looking for.

"Over here!"

He reached down and pulled up a hinged handle on the floor, yanking it hard. A several metre long and wide hatch opened, and he spun it over on its hinges.

"This is a maintenance access point. They will be safe here."

"Right, get them inside, boys!" yelled Taylor.

Come on, come on, he thought. *This might actually work.*

"Set the timers for five minutes."

"Five? Cutting that a little fine, aren't we?"

"Jafar said the machine needs three minutes to fire up once the power is going. We have no idea when that will happen, so I want as short a fuse as possible, Jones."

"We could just detonate remotely?"

"No, we can't risk it. If we die trying to make it out of here, or the signal somehow gets jammed, it'll be all over. These nukes going off is the number one priority. Us getting out alive is insignificant by comparison. If we can, we will."

"Well, aren't you a joy to be with today?"

"Hey, this isn't on me. I didn't turn up to Earth on this fucking monstrosity to try and end humanity. Find Demiran, and take it up with him."

"I intend to."

Taylor looked up to see the smile had gone, and he was

being deadly serious. He patted Jones on the shoulder and stood up beside him.

"We'll get the bastard, and we'll get him together, unless these nukes fry him. We can only hope."

"No, it can't be that easy. Someone like Demiran, he won't go down like this. We may destroy his ship, his fleet, and even his army, but when it comes down to the bastard himself, it's gonna be a job for our own hands."

Taylor could see the bitter hatred in Jones' eyes, and he wished there was a way to console him, but only the death of Demiran would satisfy his desire.

"We're good to go."

The call came from Silva, so Taylor knew he would not need any confirmation.

"All right, let's blow this hunk of junk!" Rains shouted.

"Set the charges and be ready to move!" yelled Taylor.

"Charges...armed!" Silva called out.

"Let's go!"

Taylor was first to get moving with Jafar close by his side. In just ten seconds at a sprinting pace, they reached the bodies of the Mechs they had slaughtered. Their Reitech suits were now being used to their max, providing a rapid sprint. They reached the secret access door they had left open and thundered on through. There was no need to cover their tracks any longer. They were running for their lives.

They were nearing the end of the passageway but none

had slowed down, not even Jafar who was at their head. He hit the doorway at a full sprint and smashed the door from its hinges. It bounced off the opposite wall. Taylor was out a second later and saw Jafar barrel into a roll, hitting the wall and rolling back onto his feet. Mitch had already caught the glimpse of movement when a pulse soured down the corridor between the two of them. He ripped a grenade from his webbing, tossing it quickly at the enemy soldiers and following it with several bursts.

It forced the creatures to duck for cover, and that gave the rest of the platoon enough time to get out of Demiran's no longer secret passage.

"Keep moving! Run over them!" Taylor ordered.

Just three Mechs had targeted them, and they were directly in the path they needed to get back to the Stallion. They didn't have shields, but they still advanced shoulder to shoulder at speed as if they did. Without the shields to provide cover, they used a wall of fire to do the same job. The Mechs huddled for their lives behind a small barrier, not able to raise their bodies without being instantly killed.

Taylor and Jafar reached the barrier and leapt onto it. They hadn't stopped firing as they closed the distance, and merely put their weapons over and kept firing until all three were dead. They had stopped for just a second to ensure the job was done before continuing on at a sprint. Taylor lifted his watch to see a minute and a half had passed. They were on the home run now; the long, broad corridor that took them directly to the half wrecked room where the Stallion awaited them.

"My bird better still be there!" yelled Eddie.

Nobody responded. They all knew their survival now relied entirely on that ship and it being in the state they had left it. They kept running and hoped for the best. Taylor reached the door to the room first and stopped as he entered. He half expected to run on to a firing squad or find just empty space.

"What is it?"

Eddie pushed his way to the front.

"Oh, baby! I knew you'd be there for us!"

He turned to the others who were still in as much shock as Taylor.

"What are you waiting for? Let's get the hell outta here!"

He rushed for the Stallion with the others close behind. Jones waited at the door, pulling it shut as the last of the platoon got aboard. He turned to call that they were ready, but Eddie hadn't waited for them. The engines were roaring, and they were lifting off.

"No need for secrecy anymore, hit it!" Taylor shouted.

The craft banked quickly, and Eddie quickly cranked the power up to full. They soared out from the gaping mouth of the wreckage. Taylor looked at his watch once again. There was one minute left.

"Fuck, this is gonna be close."

"Have faith, Colonel. You've done your part. Now let

us do ours."

"We've got incoming," said Perez.

Eddie brought it up on the display,which was one of the only other things they had got working for this very situation.

"Two ships on our ass."

"What can you do?" asked Taylor.

"Besides get blown to shit, not a lot. We have no weapons working, no counter measures, nothing."

Taylor shook his head.

"No God damn way. We didn't get off that thing to die now."

"I don't know what else we can do. They're gaining on us, and there ain't nobody else left to help us out."

Taylor dipped his head and thought about it for a moment. He turned and looked at Jones.

"Get the loading doors open!"

Jones didn't understand what he was saying but only hesitated for a second before rushing to the back of the craft. The larger double doors at the rear were almost as wide as the fuselage and allowed for the loading of large crates. He pushed the doors open to be met by a pulse rushing towards him. Rains banked at the last second, and it smashed into the doorway, sending hot debris burning into his armour, but saving his life.

"We've got a problem here!"

Taylor rushed to the entrance and lifted his rifle to give

a quick burst. Several others joined in, but what little fire they managed to hit the enemy ship with seemed to have no effect. Their fire was returned with a pulse that flew right through the doors and hit the roof of the Stallion. Debris smashed over the platoon, but their armour saved them from the shrapnel.

Before Taylor could get up, another pulse rushed through the opening, striking three of the soldiers and killing them instantly. It ripped through the length of the Stallion until it reached the cockpit. The core of the pulse hit Perez in the back and pierced through his front plate. Shrapnel was thrown around the cockpit as it did.

"Fuck!" Eddie screamed.

He recovered to look over at Perez and could see his co-pilot was already dead. Taylor looked over the dead and felt more pissed off than ever.

"Grenades!"

He pulled the two he had left and twisted the fuses.

"You'll need a short timing, so wait three seconds before you throw!"

He turned back and threw the two out of the door. The tiny high explosive devices vanished from sight immediately and blew almost as quickly. One missed the two enemy ships entirely, and the other struck nearby, forcing the pilot to take evasive action. Jones could see it might work and did the same.

"Come on! Everything you have!"

The rest of the platoon threw out their grenades, and the sixth was a direct hit on the engines, making one of the enemy ships slow to beyond range. The grenades kept going until Blinker came to the door with the very last one.

"Make it count," said Taylor.

He lifted the grenade to his mask, pretended to kiss it, and tossed it out the door. The blast struck near the cockpit of the enemy fighter and blasted the mirrored glass open. The pilot veered off for a second before recovering.

"God damn it, fuck!" Blinker cried out.

Taylor could now seethe pilot who wore a thin Mech power suit. His helmet was cracked from the blast, and he was lining up for a final run which would see them all dead.

"Fuck this!"

Taylor leapt from the storage doors and activated his boosters. He surged towards the fighter. Jones and the others watched in amazement as he hit the prow of the fighter and slid around to the cockpit, grasping the rim of the damaged glass.

"You crazy son of a bitch," said Jones.

They watched as he jumped in through the open glass and held his rifle against the creature's body, firing six shots on full auto. The creature slumped back dead. Taylor climbed off its corpse and leapt from the fighter. Rains lowered the power and banked to see the Gezgen K'til, as Taylor floated towards them. He used his boosters to clumsily return and bounce off the walls. Jones helped him stand steady and had just enough time to shake his head in amazement before the view from the cockpit lit up from a blast. They looked up to see a massive explosion tear through the K'til.

"Yes, you mother fuckers!" Blinker shouted.

He could not hold himself back and continued with the expletives as the others roared in excitement. Further eruptions ran along the edge of the K'til, and huge segments were blown off the vessel. For a full minute, they all stood watching, and then the most unthinkable happened. Lights pulsed over the hulking ship, and a noise began pulsating from it, like a massive power source increasing in strength. Their faces turned to stone.

"What the hell is that?" Taylor gasped.

He turned to Jafar to see the same icy fear in the creature's face.

"No, how? How can they still do this? You said it would work!"

He grabbed Jafar by the armour on his chest and hauled him in close.

"How is this happening?"

Jafar did not respond or fight back. He had nothing more to say.

"Fuck!" Taylor turned back to look at the K'til. A huge centre section began to open, revealing a massive pulsating light that could only be the weapon and the source of the sound they were hearing.

"What can we do?" he asked.

"What more can we do? We just hit them with everything we had."

Taylor slumped down in one of the seats and dropped his head into his hands.

"It's all over. We gave it everything, and still we lose."

No one had an answer. There was no way to soften the blow of realising that all they knew on Earth were going to be destroyed in less than three minutes. Just when all hope appeared lost, Rains' voice broke the silence.

"Look!"

Taylor did not get up. He couldn't imagine anything could improve the scenario. Instead, Jones rushed to the cockpit to receive the news.

"My, God, the Washington. She's got power!"

Taylor heard the words and shot up from his seat, rushing to join the two officers. He got to the cockpit to first witness the grizzly sight of Perez's body in the co-pilot's seat, and his blood splattered across the controls in front of him. He quickly turned his attention away to what was before them. As Jones had said, the engines of the their flagship, the Washington, were firing up.

"Can we get a message to Huber?" asked Taylor.

"Negative, we haven't got comms, and I doubt they do either."

"What have they got?"

"Probably just what we can see, engines. They wouldn't have had time to get anything else going. It's a miracle they're even moving so quickly after the EMP."

The Washington began to edge forward and gained speed at a steady pace, but Taylor could see the silhouettes of objects, seeming to be dropping from her hull.

"What's that?"

Eddie squinted to look.

"Life pods. They don't have any power, but enough oxygen to keep the crew alive for a day or two."

"They're evacuating but still going forward? What is Huber doing?" asked Jones.

"The only thing he can. The Washington is the only weapon we have left."

"But you just said the weapons were..."

Jones stopped as he realised what Taylor was saying.

"Huber's gonna ram the K'til, and he's getting everyone off that he can."

Taylor nodded.

"God, almighty!"

They watched as dozens of pods dropped from the Washington and were left floating in space. The pulsating light and sound of the K'til's Planet Killing weapon was uncomfortably loud now and was forcing them to shout to hear each other. Jafar stepped up to join them and could barely squeeze into the cockpit to see.

"Admiral Huber, will he be safe?"

Taylor shook his head.

"A Captain goes down with his ship. Huber will be at the helm until the end."

"A brave man."

"Yes, and he may well have just saved humanity from extinction."

They watched the last few pods leave the Washington, and its speed increased as it rushed towards the K'til. The massive carrier was still tiny compared to the huge super weapon of a ship. Taylor looked at his watch, praying they had enough time.

"One minute to go."

The rest of the platoon sat anxiously in the ship. Only the three officers and Jafar could see what was about to unfold. A few enemy ships that had regained power had cottoned on to what was happening and were moving to intercept the Washington. Pulses smashed into her hull, but it was not enough to stop her.

"Good luck to you," said Taylor.

The human flagship soared towards the opening at the core of the enemy weapon with ever increasing speed.

"Thirty seconds!" yelled Jones.

The noise was almost deafening, and they barely heard him.

The Washington pierced the light and vanished completely from sight into the K'til. The deafening pulse died almost instantly, and cracks began to appear in the hull of the Planet Killer. The light faded completely from it, and the hull began to prise apart. They watched as the monster of a vessel was torn in half and split at its core.

"He did it," Taylor said quietly.

He turned around and shouted it again for all to hear. Rains slumped back in his seat and sighed in relief. It was too soon for celebrations when he sat next to the body of a dead friend, but he at least managed a smile.

CHAPTER SIX

Taylor was speechless for five minutes as he watched the two parts of the K'til were drawn in towards Earth and broke through the atmosphere. Several of the enemy ships that had regained power followed. There was not a single remainder of the Washington to be seen, but everyone could see the evidence of her efforts.

"That thing is gonna land hard when it hits land," Eddie said.

"No, those ships are going to assist," replied Jafar.

"What do you mean assist?"

"They'll use their own power to reduce the speed and impact of the K'til."

"Why?"

"Because Demiran is onboard," said Taylor sternly.

"So?" snapped Eddie.

"Because those who don't make an effort to assist their

Lord will feel his wrath, should he still survive."

"Yes," added Jafar.

"There must be thousands of Mechs aboard that thing too," continued Jones.

"And you think they can break the fall of something that massive?" Eddie asked.

"Enough to save those aboard, yes. But the K'til will never fly again."

Power was being quickly restored to those ships around them now, but clearly many still did not have access to weapons. Most of the enemy ships made a beeline for Earth to follow their leader. They passed the monstrous Earth Defence Grid lying lifeless and unable to stop them.

"We've stopped the weapon, and they're stranded here now, but we've got a long road ahead."

"We've beaten them on Earth before. We'll do it again," replied Jones.

"This battle is over. Eddie, get us back on firm ground."

"Yes, Siree, batten down the hatches because we're going home!"

* * *

The Stallion landed hard, bouncing on the landing strip, but they quickly came to a halt and were relieved to once again be on home soil. Jones pushed open the damaged doors, with the help of Jafar, and stood aside to allow

Taylor through first. He looked around to see the base was in absolute chaos. Fighters, Stallions, and others cargo ships were scattered all over. Larger ships had put down near the hangars. Fire trucks were trying to put out what they could, and medics and doctors were treating wounded at make shift aid points. A line of body bags lay across the way beside one of the buildings. They were the only things laid out tidily with respect.

"Colonel! Colonel Taylor!"

He turned to see General White and his entourage approaching. They were all armed and armoured with the same Reitech equipment he wore.

"Is the base under attack, Sir?"

"Uhh... no. This is precautionary only. We have no idea what to expect. Communications have been down with the fleet for some time, and we are only now getting reports through of what happened. Enemy ships have entered the atmosphere and seem to be putting down somewhere over Africa or Europe. What the hell happened up there?"

"It's a long story. But the short version is that the mothership was taken down when Admiral Huber rammed it with the Washington. It's broken into two sections and has come down to Earth."

White's eyes widened.

"And the lack of communication? From down here it looked like both fleets just went dead. My experts tell me some kind of EMP."

"Exactly that, Sir."

"Okay, so let me get this straight. We won up there. Their fleet is now stranded somewhere on Earth?"

Taylor nodded.

"Well, the last thing I ever wanted to see was those bastards step foot here again, but it could have gone a whole lot worse. This Planet Killer weapon, is it done with?"

Taylor turned to Jafar for confirmation.

"Absolutely. The Gezgen K'til was the weapon, and that has gone."

White took in a deep breath and relaxed. He needed to hear the information from a reliable source before he could really take it in.

"What now, Sir?" asked Taylor.

"That's not my decision to make. They have not landed on our soil. It is for higher powers to decide that. Right now, my priority is getting these wounded seen to. I'm glad to see you made it through, Colonel."

"What are our orders?"

"Stand down, rest. You've been through hell. We have plenty of marines to get to work here. There will be a briefing at 0800 hours that I expect you to attend. Until then your time is your own."

"Thank you, Sir."

White had just left when Taylor heard his name yelled once again. It was Parker rushing towards him. Her pace slowed as she saw the bodies being carried from their Stallion. She looked at him, checking he was okay.

"You did it?" she asked.

"No, Huber did it. Our nukes went off but didn't get the job done."

"I'm afraid that's not how we saw it."

Taylor looked passed Parker to see Vega, the Washington's XO. The man had never liked him, but that dislike seemed to have washed away.

"We picked up a lot of the drop pods after the blast," Eli added.

Vega paced forward to shake Taylor's hand. He was shocked but accepted as the Captain continued.

"We were doing everything to get power back when the Planet Killer began to cycle that weapon up. We could see it but were powerless to do anything. We figured we had just a couple of minutes, but it wasn't enough. Then a massive blast tore through the ship. Not enough to destroy it, but they lost power to the weapon and had to begin the cycle again several minutes later. In that time,we had got power to the engines."

"What are you saying?"

"That you delayed the weapon for maybe five minutes, enough for our engineering crews to get the ship back on her feet for one last run. Huber ordered all crew off and remained at the manual controls until the very end. The Washington may have destroyed that thing, but it would never have been possible if it were not for you and your people."

Taylor could see Jones' platoon had been listening in. Their efforts had not been wasted, and the deaths of three of their comrades had not been in vain, but the sombre tone remained until Eddie finally felt the need to break it.

"So the long and short of it is, we whooped 'em again?"

Taylor had to smile.

"See to the dead and wounded. After that you have the night to yourselves. The battle for the Solar System is over. Tomorrow the second Battle for Earth begins. Get some rest and be ready for it."

Parker wrapped her arm around his as the others parted and led him back towards his quarters.

"You're a crazy son of a bitch, you know that? One of these days one of your crazy missions is going to be the end of you."

He turned to her and could see she jested with him. It was hard to be tough on him after the results he had achieved.

"All the crazy stunts you pull, and yet you're still alive? How do you do it?"

"I'd like to say I'm lucky. But I don't feel lucky. I ache like hell," he retorted with a smile.

They got back to his private quarters to find them just the way he had left them, spotless. All squared away and with little sign of a living inhabitant at all. He stripped off his armour and suit, throwing it all to the floor with no care in the world.

"Damn it feels good to be out of that thing."

He felt Parker's arms wrap around his shoulders from behind, and the soothing feeling of human contact made him relax immediately and feel drowsy.

"We've got one night till the shit hits the fan again," he said.

"Then let's make the most of it."

* * *

Taylor stepped out of his quarters feeling fresh and invigorated. A jeep awaited him with Captain Ryan at the wheel.

"'Morning, Colonel!"

"Glad to see you made it," he replied.

"Likewise, Sir."

"How is the Deveron?"

"She's been through hell, but she'll be back on the line in no time. Like a lift?"

"Sure."

He climbed aboard, and as the open topped vehicle got moving, he revelledin the fresh air gushing past.

"So it looks like we have a land battle on our hands?"

"Seems so."

"Most of the Navy ships are either seaborne or space

based. The Deveron is capable of operating effectively inside Earth's atmosphere with a larger payload capacity than almost anything else in the air."

"I remember."

"What I'm saying is; my crew don't want to be left out of this fight that is coming, Colonel."

"I wouldn't be so eager to get your heads blown off."

"Why, should somebody else take the risks for us? The Deveron is one of the most capable assets the Navy has, and since the death of Reyes, the crew are all to eager to stick it to the enemy."

"So this wasn't just a courtesy call?"

Ryan turned to see the comical expression on his face.

"It's good to see you alive and all that, Sir, but we want in this fight, and you're the man who can assure it."

"The enemy have come to Earth in great numbers. We're going to need any and all assets available to us. However, if you're eager to be attached to Inter-Allied, I can see to making ways for that to happen."

"Thank you, Sir. It would be much appreciated."

"You won't be thanking me when you're up to your ears in shit and having to fight them face to face."

"Been there and got the t-shirt."

Taylor thought back to their intelligence-gathering mission and remembered he was right.

"The Deveron has been good to us, both under the command of Captain Reyes and yourself. Good luck charms are hard to come by. I'll see to it that we continue to work together."

They arrived at conference hall of the base to find it guarded by twenty fully armoured marines with armoured vehicles covering all roads.

"Thank God for that. We're actually prepared for a change," whispered Taylor to Ryan.

The guards waved them through without checking IDs. There was not a marine on base who did not recognise Colonel Taylor.

"Are you authorised to be here?" he asked Ryan.

"I'm with you, aren't I?"

Taylor laughed.

"One day I'll break a rule too many, and it'll be my balls on the line."

"Haven't you already been through that?"

Taylor nodded.

"Hell, yeah."

They stepped through to see a hundred officers had gathered. Most were US Marine and Navy and with a small handful of foreign representatives. Jones was already inside as the number two for their Battalion. White spotted Taylor, and it was clearly the signal for things to get moving.

"All right, Gentlemen, Ladies, be seated!"

A display screen behind him, several metres wide, had a map of Earth up but with no annotations of information as of yet.

"First of all, I'd like to thank and congratulate the Liberty Battlegroup on a job well done. Admiral Huber gave up his life, along with so many others in defence of Earth, and as a result, we are still here today to carry the torch!"

Cheers rang out.

"Allright, all right. It should also be noted that were it not for the daring efforts of Colonel Mitch Taylor of the 2nd Inter-Allied, none of this would have been possible."

Cheers and clapping continued, but White soon drew them to a close.

"As much as we'd all like to celebrate our successes and pin medals on the uniforms of many deserving men and women, the fight isn't over."

The General got up from his seat and stood beside the map with a stick. He refused to use the laser pointers that had become the norm. He did, however, have an assistant sitting at the table ready to overlay the information as he spoke.

"This is what we do know. The so-called Planet Killer was blown into two pieces, and its descent was assisted by other enemy vessels to put down in North Africa. We're still having trouble getting satellite images as the EMP damaged many of them, but we expect that to change within the next day or so."

He lifted his cane to the map.

"The landing sites appear to be in Algeria, Tunisia, and Libya. Now you all know that these areas were ravaged during the first war, as they were some of the first targets struck. Many of the refugees who got out have never returned. So much of those countries are wastelands. This may well be the reason they chose the area, but they may not have had a choice. We cannot confirm either way at this time."

He took a deep breath, preparing himself for the next stage.

"Sergeant Jafar, who by now you are all aware of, has spent the last few hours analysing all the images and information we have to make some projection at the enemy strength."

A loud cough echoed around the room that was a deliberate interruption to make a response. It came from Lieutenant General Smith.

"Are we basing our knowledge of this enemy force on an alien who used to be not so long ago one of them? From what I understand, he was the personal bodyguard to the leader of this force."

Taylor opened his mouth to speak in defence of Jafar, but he was not given the opportunity. A fist was slammed violently down on the sturdy table, causing several present to recoil. Taylor turned to see it was Commander Kelly who he had not previously noticed.

"Sergeant Jafar is one of the finest men I have ever

met, and I will not have ill spoken of him. When this war began, my colony was left to fend for itself for many months, and yet when it came time to take it back, it was Sergeant Jafar at the front with heroes like Taylor who fought for us. Let's just remember that there are good people, and there are scumbags in all society and all walks of life. He may not be born one of us, but he is a better man than many I have known."

Kelly's booming voice and damning response to the General silenced the room. Despite having no authority on Earth, his presence and opinion held weight among many. Taylor did not feel he could respond after Kelly's praise for both him and Jafar. Kelly had one hated Taylor, just as he had hated every alien. Now they were as one fighting a common cause.

"Gentlemen, please let us keep this civil. Sergeant Jafar has proven himself time and time again. Despite my initial doubts, he has my full support, and I will not have his loyalties questioned by anyone. Now let's move on."

General Smith slumped back in his chair and avoided eye contact with both Kelly and Taylor. Taylor knew Smith wasn't a bad man or a bad officer, he just had no field experience and understanding of the way the World was changing.

"As a rough estimate, Sergeant Jafar and our intelligence analysts have put together an idea of what we are facing. They believe the enemy force could include up to five hundred thousand soldiers. Armour and numbers are unknown, but Jafar believes much of their number will have been destroyed aboard the K'til."

"Hang on, five hundred thousand soldiers?" asked Richards.

"What were you expecting?"

"I thought they came here to destroy the planet, not occupy it!"

"Jafar believes they would have intended to establish colonies on Mars and the Moon, ready to inhabit Earth when it was hospitable once more, following the strike by the K'til."

"That's some long term planning," whispered Taylor.

"We believe and hope that their access to armour and aerial support will be limited as a result of that and the damage our Navy inflicted upon them. They are stranded here, but we must not underestimate them. Yes, we have proven we can beat them in the past, but let us not forget how close we came to defeat. The World has sustained hundreds of thousands of military losses in the last few years, and God knows how many civilian."

"Then what are our intentions?" asked Smith.

"It is not for us to decide a response. World leaders and their ministers have done that. It is their belief that an immediate response to the forces in North Africa is too dangerous to engage, and that time is on our side. They believe that as a stranded army on foreign soil, every day that passes makes us stronger and them weaker."

"Jesus," whispered Taylor.

White just heard him speak and turned his attention to Taylor.

"You do not agree?"

"Hell, no, Sir. If they get a foothold on Earth, they'll gain lands and begin production of weapons and equipment quickly. Nothing good can come of their presence here. They should be hit hard, quickly, and repeatedly until they are dead. All of them."

Grunts of approval echoed the room.

"Pipe down!" White ordered. "I am inclined to agree with you, Colonel, but that is not our decision to make. This affects the entire World, and any action against the enemy will need the combined forces that every major nation has to offer."

"And how long do these leaders advise we wait?"

"A two pronged approach is being put into place. Africa is being marked out as enemy territory, and they should be contained on that continent. Rapid reaction forces are to engage all enemy presence that has landed in southern Europe and to strengthen the old defences on Israel's border with Egypt. They are to be kept inside Africa."

"What are the human numbers still on the continent?" asked Taylor.

"The estimated population of the entire continent since the war is less than a hundred million. Several operations to recover that population to safer lands are already underway, but we simply can't save everyone."

"So we defend the borders and then what? Wait?" asked Kelly.

"For one year, that is the plan agreed to by the United Nation of Earth, andtherefore we must abide it. One year to strengthen our forces and prepare for the battle to end it all."

"Preparation? Is that not what we have been doing ever since we pushed them out of this Solar System?" asked Kelly. "Are you to trying to tell me that we are not ready?"

"I am sorry, but you are preaching to the wrong man. I said this day would come, and all of us here knew it, but I do not control military budgets."

The room was silent as they all considered the prospect of a whole year with enemy occupation once more. It was starting to set in that they could not argue with the decision.

"Okay, so this is how it's gonna be," said Taylor. "You mentioned enemy elements in Southern Europe. That must now be our priority, as it is something we can deal with."

White nodded in appreciation for Taylor taking the heat off him.

"The enemy move fast. We know that from the last war. A few vessels put down on the south coast of Spain, Italy, and a few islands of Greece, as well as a number of other locations in the Mediterranean. It's pretty damn clear this war isn't going to be fought on American soil. We had it the lightest last time, and it looks like we're lucky enough to see that again. It means our civilians are safe. The European Union Army Chief has already requested assistance from both the United States and the South American Union and Canada to deploy forces immediately to the Mediterranean. Middle East and Far East forces are already amassing in Israel, Jordan, and Saudi Arabia to counter the threat from Egypt."

"Bet they're really happy about that," replied Ryan.

White looked up to see the Navy Captain standing behind Taylor. He recognised him quickly and refrained from silencing him.

"Right now, the border disputes between the Middle Eastern countries are a storm in a tea cup compared to what's coming, and I believe they see it the same way. Hostilities in that part of the world reduced significantly during and after the last war. Seems they just needed a mutual enemy to bring 'em together."

A few laughs rang out, but many were still too concerned with their own situations.

As for our own operations, the Navy is deploying four battlegroups to the Mediterranean to guard the waters around North Africa. The US Marine Corps is to deploy three divisions to the same area, along with another two from the Army. Their task is to work alongside local forces to find and destroy all enemy forces who made it to the continent, and then defend the borders until we are ready for a full scale invasion into North Africa."

"Great, when do we leave?" asked Taylor.

"For you, today, core elements of the 5th Marine Regiment depart for Southern Italy in five hours, under the command of Colonel Harney. Your Battalion will be part of that task force. You will receive landing instructions and enemy positions live en route. At this stage, there is little else to discuss, so I suggest those engaged for this mission leave now and prepare for departure. Good luck."

Taylor pushed back his chair and left without another word. It pleased him to be getting into the fight, but their leaders lack of initiative to bring the invasion to a quick end was demoralising.

"Can you give me a lift to my unit?" he asked Ryan.

"Sure thing."

"Is the Deveron ready to go?"

"There's still work to be done, but..."

"Is she ready or not?"

"Yes, Sir."

"All right, I'm having you attached to 2nd Inter-Allied on a more permanent basis. The Deveron hasn't got the capacity for the whole Battalion, so we'll need a few other ships, but I'll choose to take her any day."

They leapt in the vehicle. Jones rushed to the side and jumped in as they tore off across the base.

"You really buying that shit about leaving the enemy alone for a year?" he asked.

"I don't know. We all want to see them ended, but we shouldn't be hasty to underestimate them. The last time we did that it cost us many lives."

They reached the Battalion's parade ground to find Silva had everyone assembled and ready as if he had been expecting their arrival. The officers were huddled around discussing something of great importance out of earshot of the grunts. Taylor leapt out and immediately paced up to the Sergeant Major as he called the Battalion to attention.

"Something big happening, Sergeant Major?"

"We're going to war, Sir."

"And why would you think that?"

He was expecting someone had already leaked the news of the mission, but it was not the response he got.

"Because the alien sons of bitches are back, and we're always first to go at 'em, Sir."

Taylor could do nothing but nod in agreement, but he turned to see that the officers clearly knew more than that.

"At ease, Sergeant."

He stepped up onto one of the small walls surrounding a barrack room to address the Battalion, without stepping in to discover the manner of the officers' meeting.

"You all know the second battle for Earth has begun. It began the moment those alien bastards came back through the Gateway. They came to destroy life on our planet. They failed. Just as they failed to conquer the planet the first time around, I want nothing less this time!"

Cheers sounded from across them all. The fear of the aliens had subsided. No one wanted to die, but they were now all more confident of victory than ever before.

"You have three hours before we assemble at landing zone B. You know what you have to do. Draw any new equipment you need, ensure everything you have is on the top line, and know that we aren't going to see our homes again until this is done and over! Fall out and get to it!"

"That really the case, we're in combat till this ends? Not exactly the way I heard it from the General."

"What is planned and the way it goes down are two very different things, Charlie."

"They are when you pick and choose how and which orders to obey," he replied with a cheeky smile.

The other officers of Inter-Allied joined them, and he could see they had already known the news almost as quickly as he had. He glared at them until they finally caved in and admitted it.

"Friend of mine in the 5th told me we were heading to Italy a few hours back," stated Jackson.

"Well nice to know somebody is kept in the loop."

"What do you mean?"

"We're heading for Italy merely to sweep and clear the coast and then hold there to ensure the enemy does not cross the Mediterranean in any great numbers."

"For what reason? Shouldn't we be hitting them now while they're in disarray?" asked Ota.

"Damn right, but that's not our call. Grab your gear, and be sure you're ready for a prolonged deployment because we're heading east to sweat to death in the baking heat."

"Hell, after almost dying in that cold and fighting through it last time, it'll be a pleasure," replied Jones.

Taylor turned and walked away, signalling Jones to join him.

"I'll remind you of that when we're slogging it through the desert; when your lips are cracked, and your vision starts to blur. You'll pray you were up to your ears in snow again," replied Taylor.

"Well, aren't you a merry one this morning?"

"I just don't like this. This is a gamble which could cost us dearly."

"You think they'll get established and have a foothold on Earth?"

"Yes, they pretty much managed it before. I can't help but feelour people are hoping if we leave them alone, they'll fix up their ships and just take off."

"You think are that naive?"

"Yes, I do. I know they are."

* * *

It was not far from midday by the time the 2nd Inter-Allied had assembled on the strip. The dead and wounded from the day before had been removed and taken care of, but much of the wreckage still lay about the scene; spaceships as large as frigates had been forced to put down on any spare ground and wouldn't be moving again any time soon. Much of the base was beginning to look like a scrap yard, and like a scrapyard, mechanics were salvaging any parts they could from the wrecked craft to get going what they could.

The smell in the air was still of burnt electrical components where pulses had done so much damage to everything which had returned. Jones approached, and he still wore the battle-scorched armour that took the impact and saved his life in the Stallion the day before. Only his uniform had been changed and was almost new.

"You seriously going to wear that thing?" asked Taylor.

"Hey, if this isn't lucky, what is? I'll have some techs do repairs when we get the time, but this armour is staying right where it belongs."

He wasn't going to argue. The fact they werestill breathing was astonishing. He didn't want to tempt fate or risk losing the cast iron morale his unit were so famous for.

"This leader of theirs, Demiran. He seems to be pretty pissed with us. Seems to me he'll go to the ends of the Earth to end us."

"Seems so, what about it?"

"Reckon he was the one who attacked Red 1 and forced us to leave Chandra behind?"

Taylor was quiet for a moment. He wasn't going to admit he'd had the same thought, for such personal revenge could destabilise the unit. He knew all too well what the effects of getting personal were.

"Yeah, I suppose there is a good chance."

"Mmmm."

"What?"

"I'm just thinking what I'm gonna do to that bastard when we finally meet."

Taylor rested his hand on the Captain's shoulder.

"Now you remember what happened last time, when we took down Karadag. You disobeyed my orders, and you compromised us all with your anger and frenzied attack."

Jones dipped his head in shame.

"If we get a chance at that son of a bitch, we're gonna do it right, you hear?"

"Sure thing. I was a wreck back then. I wasn't thinking straight."

"I know, forget about it. It's been and gone now. Important thing is we toasted the bastard."

Taylor could see Jones was deep in thought once again.

"What is it?"

"You know how we feel about Demiran, how much we all want our revenge. Surely he must feel the same for the death of Karadag. After all, they were more than just allies. They were family."

"True, but let's not forget who started this fight?"

"And if the circle of revenge simply continues one after the other for both sides?"

"Well, I guess we'll just have to kill enough of them that it ends."

"It's not a bad idea."

Genocide? Taylor thought.

He'd never considered it a possibility for a civilized people, not until now. He turned to look at Jafar, reminding himself of what the aliens had the potential to be. He tried to humanise them to keep his own humanity.

"Enough of this, it's time."

"No send off speech by the General?" asked Jones.

"No, he's busy arranging resources for the next wave. If this year-long preparation really is as he suggests, then they have a whole lot of work ahead of them."

"Why though? Why not just amass everything we have and go in now? Hit them before they can establish themselves."

"I suppose nobody wants to gamble with the whole World. To take them on we will need a vast army, with all major powers in the world contributing. Imagine if that failed. Imagine 1943, and the allies threw everything in against the Germans and lost. Just try and imagine the World if that had happened. I may not like this strategy.

It shows a caution we are not used to as field officers, but it is right for the human race. Who could make that gamble?"

Jones was taken aback by his assessment and gave it some real consideration and reflection.

"Yeah, that's a reality kick in the head."

Taylor laughed.

"Don't worry about it, ain't gonna happen."

"Guess it's your time for a speech then?"

"Haven't I given one already?"

Jones shrugged his shoulders. Taylor turned to the Battalion who were formed up with all their gear, awaiting orders. He was all out of speeches.

"Load up and be ready to kick some ass!"

"Go, go, go!" Silva shouted, as they stood stunned for a second.

The troops turned and rushed for the ships. The Deveron was reserved for Taylor and Jones' Company. Two other ships lay alongside Ryan's. They were both civilian freighters designed for high-speed haulage across the globe. Neither were armed or armoured in anyway.

"Better hope we don't hit any trouble in the air," said Jones.

"We'll be fine. The enemy is probably still in a complete mess, and we have been guaranteed fighter escort when we cover the Atlantic."

"Just as well," replied Ryan, "because our guns still aren't working either. The chips and electronics on our missile bays are fried, and the gun positions got hammered during the last couple of fights. Just be thankful that at least we have speed on our side."

"Compared to what?"

"Compared to those rust buckets," he replied, pointing to the other two ships.

"Is this really the best they could get for us?" asked Jones.

"At this short notice, I guess so. The proper kit is probably being reserved for the big operation."

"In a year? Get real. We've been given the junkers."

"Hey!" yelled Ryan."The Deveron may be a little rough right now, but she's still the best ship operating inside the atmosphere, and don't you forget it!"

Jones shrugged in an apology as they stepped up the ramp. Taylor slapped his hand on the fuselage as he passed through the door.

"Yep, this girl has done us proud."

Taylor followed Ryan up to the bridge. He had gotten so used to long distance travel in space that he had begun to think of setting up home, but Italy was just a few hours away by air.

"We still not got coordinates?" asked Ryan.

"Nope, you're to follow the 5th Marine ships, and we'll be given operational details as and when they are available and needed."

Ryan looked out to the Marine regiment mounting up. Their ships were brand new off the line and gleaming, the next generation on from the Deveron.

"Don't let their good looks fool you, Colonel. They're bigger than this girl with a bigger payload and more guns, but we can still outrun 'em any day."

The 5th Marine Regiment had dozens of ships and was beginning to lift off, despite the fact no orders had been passed on to Taylor.

"No take off authorisation or orders?" asked Ryan.

Taylor shook his head with a smile.

"The 5th haven't seen action in some time and are eager for glory. They won't share any information unless they absolutely have to. You just tail them till we know otherwise. If they want to lead the way into the enemy, let 'em. Makes a change. It's usually us having to take the flack."

"Power up and lift off."

Ryan felt awkward not having any coordinates to give to his crew, and he refused to tell them to follow the 5th Marine.

"Plot a course for Southern Italy, Cozenza."

Taylor turned in surprise. He'd never been to the country and was surprised to hear Ryan even know the name of any towns there.

"That place mean something to you?"

"I knew a girl there once," he replied.

"I bet you did."

Jafar stepped up onto the bridge. Taylor wasn't sure if he was going to join them at all and must have got on just before the doors shut.

"Good of you to join us."

"I told them I will help all I can, but where you go, I go."

"How'd they take it?"

"Why should you care?"

"Mmm... fair enough. Good to have you with us. This ain't the strike I was expecting, but atleast we're heading in the right direction."

CHAPTER SEVEN

"2nd Inter-Allied, you are to report to Italian Authorities in Naples to establish a base of operations south of the city. The coordinates are being sent to you now. 5th Marine is continuing on to Potenza where they will engage any enemy presence."

Ryan looked around and to see the pissed off expression on Taylor's face.

"Looks like we just got benched."

"I said they wanted their glory."

"Let 'em have it. You have nothing to prove, and chilling out and taking in a few rays can't do any of us any harm."

"They're going in hot headed, and without intel on the area and enemy deployments, not smart. I want as much info as you can get me in the next twenty minutes on enemy movements. Something tells me we're gonna be called for soon."

"And this order to head for Naples?"

"Go with it. We'll be a short distance from the fight."

"Sir, I have an incoming transmission from Colonel Harney for you."

"Put him through," Taylor said through gritted teeth.

A projection of the Fighting Fifth Commander appeared before them.

"We're glad to have you aboard this mission, Colonel. The 5th is heading right for the enemy targets to eliminate them quickly. I understand you are accustomed to being at the head of the action, but I want you to secure the area at our backs and take it a little easy. Your people have been through enough."

"No easy life for a marine when the enemy is at our door, Sir."

"You have your orders, Colonel, good luck."

They came down quickly onto a field where Italian forces were assembling south of the city. The country had been brutally ravaged by the first war like most of the Mediterranean, and Taylor knew their military was a long way from recovering. They had mustered just a two companies at the staging area, which meant the elite 2nd Inter-Allied outnumbered the local forces they were going to assist.

The Deveron and the two other craft put down just twenty metres in front of the group of soldiers and their lightly armoured vehicles. Taylor stood and studied them from the bridge for a moment after they had made their landing.

"They're young, inexperienced," Jones finally said.

"Are you surprised? Few of their soldiers survived the last war. Most of what they can muster are barely out of training, and with few experienced officers and NCOs to see them on their way."

"I guess that's why they sent us."

Taylor turned to face the other officers of the Battalion standing at the back of the bridge awaiting his orders.

"Let's get something straight. We may be on their soil, but we are not under their command. You follow my orders or those of our own command. Commander Phillips is en route to assume HQ duties of both us and several other units in the area. I don't care if there's a General out there. This command is mine. I will not have any of our own put in harm's way because some freshman wants to make a name for himself.

"You think that's what we'll face?" asked Jones.

"Probably. Jackson, dismount and have the Battalion form up. Jones and Jafar, you're with me. We're going to meet whoever thinks they're running this thing."

Jones smiled, he could only imagine the humiliation an unsuspecting young officer was about to receive. They stepped down the ramp to find a greeting party awaiting them. The man at the centre wore the rank of Major, and he appeared to be the highest ranked among them.

"Colonel Taylor!" he shouted rather informally.

There was no salute, and he rushed up to Taylor with his hand outstretched. He quickly stopped, realising his mistake. His arm shot up into a salute, but the smile still adorned his face. He stretched his hand out once again which Taylor could not rightfully refuse.

"Colonel Taylor, it is such an honour to meet you."

The man tried to shake his hand vigorously, but the strength provided by the exosuit made for little movement. It was clear to him that they had never been equipped or trained with the Reitech gear. They had been entirely equipped from pre-war stores.

"The Immortals standing before us. I could never have imagined it! I am Major Gallo, and I welcome you to Naples."

Taylor looked out across to the Major's men who stood casually about. Many were leaning against the vehicles for the shade and few looked eager to work.

A lazy Italian? Who would have thought it?

He smiled at the sight and just refrained from saying what he saw.

"Have you boys encountered the enemy yet?"

"Uh, no, Sir. We have had a few reports of fighting breaking out further south, but we were ordered to assemble here and await further support."

"Well, we're it. Don't take this the wrong way, Major, but have you or any of your troops fought a Mech?"

"No, Sir, but we have been in training for a year and are eager to do so."

Taylor nodded and groaned in doubt.

"We are here to fight for our country, Colonel, ready and prepared."

"It is not your courage or determination I doubt, but this gear you have. When the first war started, we needed to outnumber them ten to one to stand a chance. They have superior weapons, armour, and strength to anything that we had in use at the time. If you're going to go to war with that gear, better ensure you never try and take on more than a platoon of the Mechs."

The Major was taken aback by his words. His instinct was to defend his abilities and those of his men, but his respect for Taylor stopped him. It cast a heavy shadow over his optimism.

"Then you believe we are close to useless without this equipment you have?"

"Not far short. If you had witnessed the losses I had early on in the war, you would understand where I am coming from."

"What do you suggest we do?"

"Talk to your commanders. Arrange for Reitech equipment to be issued immediately through whatever urgent operational requirement facility you have."

"Urgent operational requirement?" the Major sniggered."It's a wonder we got issued what we have. Most of it we had to find ourselves in old stockpiles. There was little remaining of my country when the enemy had gone. My family left with little more than the clothes on our backs, and came home to not much more. I wish we had access to the resources you did, but until I do, we must do the best we can."

"All right, no offence meant, Major."

Jones stepped forward to address the young Italian. He appeared to be no older than twenty and was of short and slight stature compared to the two of them. And yet he stood proud and tall. He was far too young for the rank he held, but they both knew it was a result of the war. It was a reminder of how lucky they were to have survived this far.

"We just want to see you get what you need and deserve to make it through this fight."

"Then please, do anything you can to see it happen. I have trained these men and women to the best of my ability, but my training officer was a sixty-five year old Major who was just a week from retirement when the war began. He was one of the few to make it through, after he was put in charge of seeing thousands of civilians to safety. I have no contacts to get these things, and no one to help."

"That's where you're wrong," replied Taylor. "You just got us, and we're here to make sure you get through this alive."

Taylor had expected an arrogant and self-important

officer, but instead he found himself liking the Major. He'd already decided he would make it is his mission to get them equipped and able to face the enemy as a force to be reckoned with.

"Where are you based, Major?" asked Taylor.

"You are within the borders of our base here. Much of it was destroyed during the war. We have begun rebuilding here in the last six months."

He stepped closer to whisper to the Colonel.

"My only task since getting my commission has been to begin rebuilding the base here. We have basic accommodation and training grounds for six hundred soldiers, with many more still living under temporary shelters."

Taylor stepped back to talk more plainly.

"Don't be ashamed of what you have done here. We live in difficult times, and you and your lot have had the courage to volunteer in the face of evil."

Gallo laughed hesitantly.

"We volunteered after the war was over. We never expected to fight in the next one."

Taylor laughed.

"None of us wanted it, but that doesn't make it any less necessary. You and I are here, and we have a job to do."

* * *

The day passed quickly once they had been given a plot to assemble their own billets. Taylor grew restless being sidelined by the 5th Marine Regiment, and he could sense the others felt the same. Their fear of combat had been replaced with a desire for revenge. A bloodthirsty desirehe knew had to be controlled. He sat up in his bed, realising how much he missed Parker. They could not rightfully share a bed on an operation even though she made every opportunity to do so.

Taylor stepped out of his billet into the open air. It was warm and comforting. He looked up to the stars and took great pleasure in seeing the skies so peaceful and quiet, despite the fact he knew it would not last. As he stood there in the moonlight, a voice spoke out from behind him, but he did not react for it was the soothing sound of a friend.

"You are thinking about her too."

He knew it was Charlie Jones. The British officer's stern and deep voice was unmistakeable even among his own country folk.

"We never leave anyone behind. We lost you momentarily, but we did everything in our power to get you back. What have we done to see Chandra returned home? Dead or alive, she deserves more than to be left out there."

"It's all very well, but some things are simply beyond our reach. It was a wonder we didn't lose more in Tau Ceti.

The only reason we're still here is because we weren't sent to Red 1 with her."

They both knew in their hearts that she was dead, for there was no possibility of her surviving the onslaught they witnessed.

"And maybe if we had been there, the story would have been different," replied Taylor.

"We have pulled off some miraculous things in our time together, but we are only human after all. We couldn't have made a difference down there."

They stopped and watched the stars for a moment. It was a beautifully clear night.

"We've lost a lot of friends since it began, and we'll lose many more before this is over. The end of this enemy force is in sight. Both sides must see it, but neither can nor will back down. We have to slug it out and see it through," said Taylor.

"These Italian boys, they aren't ready. Not even close."

"No, but their hearts are in it. They deserve better, better equipment, better training. I'm going to make it my mission to see that happens."

"In the middle of a war?"

"You heard our orders. After the European coastlines are clear, we're gonna be held up here for some time."

"And you think these things ever go to plan?"

Taylor laughed.

"No, but we can only hope."

* * *

Daybreak came and Taylor awoke to the sunrays beating down on his shelter and trying to cook him in his bed. It was all the incentive he needed to get to his feet and out the door. An HQ shelter had been setup with their comms officers and equipment not far from his billet. Jones was already up and at the station. He stood over an ops table, studying the information they had been provided, but there seemed little urgency to his job.

"We got any accurate information on enemy positions yet?" asked Taylor as he strode forward.

Jones nodded, pointing down to the ops table map.

"We've got positive enemy sights at three locations. However, the two reconnaissance craft sent over took heavy fire and were unable to get much info. Satellite imagery is still down also. The 5th is approaching from three positions north of Potenza to engage two of the enemy locations."

"Have they requested our assistance?"

Jones shook his head.

"Fools. I want you to keep in regular contact with the 5th. They will need our support, and I want to be ready for when that time comes."

He turned to see Major Gallo approaching on foot.

"What are your current orders?" asked Taylor.

"To hold the southern roads to Naples."

"And what does that entail?"

"We have defensive lines covering four kilometres."

"With what did you say, six hundred men?"

Gallo nodded.

"How are your defences organised?"

"We have a bunker every kilometre, and sentries roaming the spaces in between."

"What have you got on your eastern flank?"

"Reconnaissance regiment with armoured cars and protecting ten kilometres inland. I do not know what is beyond them."

Taylor thought about it for a moment. It reminded Jones of being back in Brest on the west coast of France - spread thin and ill equipped.

"Sir, the 5th has made contact at Buccino and north of Potenza."

Taylor turned back to the ops table, for the names meant nothing to him. As far as his knowledge of the country extended was the rough location of Rome and Naples from looking at the map that morning.

"Okay, so that's what, eighty kilometres from here?"

"About that, yes," replied Gallo.

"Have we got any idea on enemy numbers yet?"

Jafar stepped up towards them, and Gallo recoiled at the sight of him. He could see the uniform markings on his armour but still could not believe it. He looked to both

Taylor and Jones for confirmation that Jafar was for real and friendly.

"This is Sergeant Jafar and he is one of ours," Taylor said.

"But..."

"But nothing, Major."

Gallo turned to study the alien. They could all see it was the closest he had ever come to one, but it was not what he was expecting at all. The short Italian officer had to look up to see the eyes of the towering Jafar.

"Are there many more like you, fighting for us?" he asked.

"There was one, but he was lost in Tau Ceti."

"Enough, there'll be time for questions when the enemy isn't at the door."

They turned back to the map.

"The marines will have their work cut out at those two towns. Rolling hills and many narrow mountain roads. Much of the terrain is barren and without cover."

"Do you have any forces south of here?"

"Small numbers in Cosenza and extending into Sicily, but all have been ordered to setup defensive lines at their locations and await further support. The civilians from here down are being evacuated by air and sea, and above Naples they are being moved north."

"That's gonna take time."

"Yes, but not as long as you might think. The population

of my country is a shadow of its former self. So many ghost towns."

Taylor looked back to the map, which was being updated live with enemy positions throughout the Med and Africa as they came in.

"What are they doing in southern Italy? Doesn't look like they are in great numbers, and we don't have any sign of them receiving additional support as of yet. Much longer, and our fleets will ensure they are cut off completely."

"Maybe this wasn't their intended target?" asked Jones. "Seems all that could amassed in North Africa. Perhaps this was the closest they could get if their ship was severely damaged."

Lieutenant Yorath was clearly receiving new information at his comms station, and Taylor waited impatiently to hear the news.

"Sir, first recon images from the 5th are in."

"Anything useful?"

"I believe so, Sir, looks like some kind of crash site. They'll be on the table presently."

Five images popped up, and it took a few seconds for them to realise what they were looking at until Jafar finally spoke.

"That is a heavy cruiser, and it looks badly damaged."

"Then it is a crash site?" asked Jones.

"Yes."

"What can we expect from a ship of that size?"

"A thousand crew and enough equipment for them all to fight on the ground. Support ships may also have remained with them."

"All right, at least we have some idea on numbers. They must have sustained losses in the battle and probably more in that crash landing. But if their support vessels have joined them, we must assume they have their full one thousand strength or more."

"Potentially many more," replied Jafar.

He pointed to a wooded area where part had been flattened that only a key eye would have spotted.

"You think that's another crash site?"

"Or a good hiding place," added Jones.

Jafar nodded, without giving a solid answer to either of them.

"Where are these two sites in relation to the 5th's current position?" asked Taylor.

"The map is being updated as we speak," added Yorath.

Taylor looked over the map and could see the three elements of the 5th Marine were advancing on the heavy cruiser and had already passed the other potential landing site.

"They haven't seen it."

"Idiots," replied Jones.

"Yorath, mark the second potential crash site and warn them immediately!"

Before the Lieutenant could react, he received frantic

new calls across the radio.

"Sir, 5th Marine is reporting enemy advances north of their position."

"Christ, they're getting surrounded," said Jones.

Taylor looked to the map again.

"Muro Lucano, that's where the second ship is. They must have moved south quickly."

"Heavy woodland in that area. It would cover their movements well. No idea of telling how many of them are there."

"Have they requested our assistance?" asked Taylor.

"No, Sir," replied Yorath.

"Well, tough shit. They're getting it anyway."

"What about our orders to defend this area?"

"We can do both, Jones. Captain Jackson, I want you to join Major Gallo's defensive lines, a platoon per position at each kilometre as Gallo setup. The rest of us are heading to Muro Lucano."

He looked up to see Eddie Rains had just woken and was stretching as he came out of his billet.

"Rains!"

The Lieutenant jumped at the bellowing of his name.

"Are the copters ready to go?"

He paced up casually and confidently.

"Unloaded last night, Sir. We've been good to go since we hit this country."

"Good, then fire 'em up. There are marines who need

our help."

Captain Ryan spoke up from where he had been standing by the ops table.

"What do you want us to do?"

"Right now, your priority should be to get your weapon systems online. With those active, you'll be able to provide some valuable air cover."

"That could take a couple of days, easy."

"It'll take what it'll take, and see to getting any weapons you can installed on the other two ships."

"They're just civilian transports."

"Not anymore. I'm not expecting miracles, but anything you can get on them to give them a fighting chance will help."

"I'll do what I can."

"That's all I ask."

He turned back to Jones.

"Get the other three companies assembled, I want to be in the air in fifteen minutes!"

He acknowledged as his lifted him comms unit and began barking his orders. Taylor was already carrying everything he needed. When so close to the enemy, he only removed his armour when sleeping, and even then kept it close to hand. He looked back at the map to study the location.

"They went headlong into this. Harney wants to make his name."

"He want's to be a great hero like you," replied Gallo.

Taylor looked up into the eyes of the Major. He didn't like being called a hero. It was an honour he found hard to accept when he had lost so many friends.

"I may have made some kind of name, but it wasn't by carelessly throwing myself at the enemy. I have survived this long by using my head."

Gallo clung to his every word, and Mitch could tell he was being treated as the officer's personal hero and role model.

"What are my orders?"

"You are to carry on as you have been, only with the support of one of my companies. They'll provide valuable support to your defences."

"And will you coordinate the operation from here?"

"No, I do not leave others to do the fighting."

"But is it not right to have somebody to coordinate remotely?"

"Yes, but that is not for me to do. Commander Phillips is en route to handle that."

"Let us join you. We're ready."

Taylor took a deep breath as he thought it over. He was deeply divided on the subject.

The support would be welcome, but they'll prove little worth in their present state.

"I like you, Gallo, and it will be an honour to fight beside you. But I will not throw you to the wolves. I know what it's like to face the enemy with the equipment you are using, and it is an experience I would not wish for any man. Hold your positions and bide your time. There will plenty of opportunity for you to get a hand in this war yet."

Gallo accepted his orders and his advice without hesitation.

"One last thing. You may be the second highest rank within our two forces, but my troops answer to me. This is not a personal matter. My officers have more combat experience than anyone I know. Trust them and work with them."

The young officer agreed quickly, and Taylor could see he was glad to have some of the responsibility lifted from his shoulders. "I'm outta here, Major."

"Good luck."

"Thanks."

He took one last look at the map, checked his Mappad device was working and updated, and grabbed his rifle. He shook his head as he thought more about Harney's blunder. On the one hand he wanted to smack the Colonel in the face, and on the other he just wanted to get his fellow marines out alive.

He reached the landing pads that had been cleared. It was little more than a dusty plain with the copters lined up and a few instant shelters beside them. Their engines were already fired up, and the three companies were clambering aboard the dozen birds. Eddie was back to his old self, wearing his ragged clothing and shunning the body armour and suit he had been provided.

"Damn it feels good to be fighting in the fresh air again!" he yelled as Taylor approached.

"Can't argue with that."

Though the air wasn't especially fresh. The copter engines were kicking up dust and debris that was filling his nostrils and throat, but he'd still prefer it to the full helmets. He looked at his watch, just eight minutes had passed, and the last few marines were climbing aboard. He was the last to step up onto Rains' copter. He lifted his comms unit.

"All aboard, let's move out!"

Rains was quick to respond, and the dust cloud seemed to explode beneath them as the power was increased and they lifted off. Taylor stood at the open side door to watch their departure. Gallo was watching them for the ground. Taylor knew he had made the right decision to leave the Italian soldiers behind.

They would be like lambs to the slaughter.

He stepped up to cockpit to see the view ahead.

"Colonel Taylor, meet Luke Wiseman, my new co-pilot."

"It's an honour, Sir."

"Yeah, well you serve with us for a few weeks and see if you still think as much. We get the shit missions, and there ain't no payoff or bonuses."

Rains burst out into laughter. It took just ten minutes for them to reach the outskirts of Muro Lucano.

"That's their landing zone, we reckon!" Taylor pointed.

"Aren't we going to assist the 5th?"

"We have to neutralise all enemy targets to the north before jumping in and making the same mistake they do. Take us in close. I want to come down right on their heads. With any luck, we'll be sweeping south in no time."

"You think that's a good idea? We don't have any idea what's down there."

"They must have committed most of their forces to drive south, so there can't be a lot. Time is not a luxury we have right now."

The copters came in low and skimmed the treetops before roaring out over the area of collapsed trees. Within it lay an enemy frigate in seemingly perfect condition. Jafar leaned out over the side for a good look.

"They landed her deliberately!"

Taylor knew there was no more time to waste analysing the situation.

"All companies move in!"

He reached the door and leapt out between the gap Jafar had left. His alien comrade was quick to jump after him. Their boosters activated and brought them to a quick and safe landing on the ground just fifty metres from the enemy vessel. Only two Mechs stood guard at the entrance ramp to the ship, and they were overwhelmed by gunfire before they could get more than a couple of shots off.

Taylor was moving towards the ramp the second he hit the ground. Six more of the soldiers rushed out from the doorway and were hit by automatic fire by thirty of Jones' troops. They didn't stand a chance against the overwhelming odds. He reached the ramp and could see no sign of further movement. He looked up at the vast space ship that was four times the size of the Deveron. He doubted there were many enemy left inside.

"All units, deploy charges by sector at ten metres intervals, two minute timers. Rendezvous at the clearing one click south for immediate recovery."

The platoon he was with moved up and placed the magnetic charges onto the hull. Individually, they could only do minimal damage, but with two-dozen or more, he calculated it would be enough to cripple the vessel and likely kill anyone onboard.

"Taylor to Yorath, we have confirmed enemy presence at Muro Lucano. Call in a strike on our coordinates in fifteen minutes."

"Affirmative, Sir."

"You think that'll be necessary?" asked Jones.

"This will disable them for now, but I don't want anyone surviving or them having equipment they can recover. It's the only way to be sure."

Jones wasn't going to argue with that. He would

happily see all evidence of the enemy obliterated beyond recognition.

"Let's move it, haul ass!"

They rushed from the clearing at a quick pace into the nearby trees and beyond until they reached the edge, bursting out into open ground where the copters were awaiting them. As Taylor reached Rains' position, the explosion erupted at their backs. A loud boom echoed for kilometres all around. Jones nodded in satisfaction.

"Another one bites the dust," he whispered to himself.

"We need to move fast. That can't have gone unnoticed by whatever forces headed south!" Taylor called out.

"It's always nice to make an entrance," replied Jones.

They leapt aboard and were in the air within a few minutes. Their feet had barely touched the ground. They were just ten kilometres north of the Fighting Fifth now; Taylor only prayed they were in time to help. He watched with bated breath as they passed over one hill to the next. They kept low to hide their position, but it also meant they had little visibility on what was ahead. As they passed a crest, it opened up into a broad valley, and they were hit with what resembled a fireworks display. Pulses and tracer fire were going in all directions.

"My, God," said Rains.

Mech forces were on both sides of the valley, with troops of the 5th Marine Regiment in the basin fighting for their lives. They could already make out lines of dead from both sides scattered throughout the valley where each side had fought desperately to gain ground.

"Put us down, now!" Taylor shouted.

"Right here?"

"Now!"

He turned to Jones.

"We have to take on this northern assault now, or they aren't gonna make it!"

The copters came to an abrupt halt.

"Why the hell didn't we know about this?"

"Either they were too proud to call it in, or couldn't!" yelled Taylor.

I know Harney wants his glory, but I doubt the Colonel would compromise so many lives for it. That begs the question, has the enemy found new ways to jam communications?

It was a disheartening thought whatever the answer, but there was no more time to think about it."

"Go!" he ordered the troops closest to the door. He rushed after them and leapt out. He quickly found himself descending onto a burst of gunfire from a Mech weapon and pushed his shield down enough to take the impact and land safely on his feet. He already knew the tactics sucked, but they had no time to plan and conduct a better strategy.

He and Jones' platoon landed amongst ten Mechs who had been advancing over the crest of the valley edge and were caught completely by surprise. He fired quickly with his rifle, killing one just a second after hitting the ground. Another pulse smashed into his shield, twisting it on his arm and almost breaking the joint. The support of his exosuit was all that saved him. He spun around and threw the shield at his attacker with all his strength.

"Son of a bitch!"

The weighty metal shield smashed into the Mech and launched it off its feet. Seizing the opportunity,he rushed at the beast and jumped onto it. He held the barrel of his gun to its faceplate and fired a burst before it could recover. He turned to see the troops of Inter-Allied dropping all around. Many fired as they made their descent. The first Mechs they landed amongst were completely overwhelmed. He reached for his shield which had blue blood splattered over it from the burst he had just fired.

"God damn disgusting," he said as he spat out on the grass.

His mouth was full of sweat and dirt, mixed with the foul iron taste of their blood.

"Ota move west, Grey to the east, Jones' Company with me. We're going forward!"

He looked down into the valley to see hundreds of Mechs. The rearmost ranks had realised what was bearing down on them, but it would do them little good. They turned to fire on Taylor's troops but were already being hit by the crossfire of the Fighting Fifth in the base of the valley.

"Let's take these bastards down quick!"

They paced forward steadily with their shields held out front and their weapons firing at every target they could find. Taylor threw two grenades as he approached the nearest Mech position and kept up his fire. Another two pulses struck his shield, and he was starting to feel the heat. It was beginning to fail under the continued blasts. He got to a sprint and rushed at the nearest creature, firing on full auto as he did. It took six shots to the chest before he crashed into it with his full weight. His weakened shield buckled under the pressure of the impact and cracked at its core.

As the alien tumbled to the ground, he saw another two behind it ready to fire on him, but Jones' Company cut them down where they stood. He used the opportunity to rush past them. The next line of creatures was fighting from a tall stonewall and firing down on the marines. Many still had their backs to the top of the valley, unaware of the new human force.

Taylor rushed at the wall and sprayed a burst across the back of one, drew his Assegai and thrust it up through the base of the spine armour of another. He spun and raised his rifle, killing another beside them. The wall of enemy succumbed to a barrage of fire from the incoming company who completely overwhelmed them.

Jones reached him, and they looked out to their flanks to see Ota and Grey were pushing forward almost as quickly. Two hundred Mechs lay dead on the hillside in just five minutes of fighting. He peered out over the wall to see the last few Mechs were being taken down by the marinesadvancing up the hill towards them. He lifted his hand to call a ceasefire and let them finish the job.

He watched as two-dozen marines made their way up the hill, and it wasn't long before he recognised Harney among them. He jumped over the wall to greet them, signalling the company to follow him. Harney's marines looked like they had been through hell. They had badly burnt and damaged armour, and many had been struck by debris and tree bursts. Harney appeared in absolute shock, but Taylor didn't know if that was from the fight or the sight of reinforcements.

"Taylor!" We have been calling for assistance for the last two hours but can't seem to get a signal through. What the hell happened here?"

"My best guess is they jammed your signal somehow. Evidently, our counter-jamming equipment isn't perfect."

"How did you know about this northern assault?"

"We discovered the possibility looking at the surveillance images."

"I saw those same images and saw nothing."

"It wasn't easy to spot."

Harney smiled in appreciation. He knew he had made a huge mistake, but Taylor was not rubbing his nose in it.

"There's still a lot of opposition on the southern ridge.

We sure could do with your assistance."

Taylor noted from that moment on, Harney was seeing him in a whole new light.

"Couldn't you get evac from here?"

"We tried, but our birds are waiting a few clicks to the west. I'm not sure if they're still okay. I sent a runner to them an hour ago but have heard nothing. Was this a targeted ambush?"

"Of a sort. The vessel south of here is a crash site. We believe their support ships landed further north to prevent any of us overrunning them while they make their retreat."

"Retreat?"

"They're amassing in North Africa. I don't believe they ever intended to put down here."

"Then they can't be that strong."

Engines roared as their copters approached from the north and put down over in the field near them among the enemy dead. Taylor knew they'd just leapt into a dangerous situation and was thankful it had paid off. He turned back to Harney.

"No, they aren't. It's prime time to bring them down. Let's move up and cut these bastards down!"

CHAPTER EIGHT

It took the combined forces of 2nd Inter-Allied and 5th Marine Regiment the rest of the day to sweep the enemy off the hilltops and back to their ship. When they finally caught sight of the stricken heavy cruiser, the sun was going down, and Taylor knew it was time to stop. Harney was by his side as they looked on at the hulking vessel which hull was part sunken below the surface.

"What now?" he asked.

"Nothing left to do until morning. We set up defences here and get what rest we can. We should arrange an aerial strike for first light."

"Why not now?"

"Well, for a start, I don't reckon it'll even be achievable, but I also want to see the result of our work and mop up any survivors before they can disperse into these hills and woods."

Taylor could see Harney didn't fully agree with his assessment and plan, but he wasn't going to argue with him after the day they had experienced. Taylor turned to Jones who had been standing close behind.

"Make it happen."

Harney nodded for his support staff to do likewise. He was happy for some responsibly to be taken off him after the near disastrous day.

"Our communications, they were down for just a few hours and then back again, what do you think is happening?"

"I guess they have a more narrow focussed and powerful machine. I doubt they'd be able to jam any larger areas, or they would have done so already."

"Seems a pretty big assumption," replied Harney.

"Only going on the intel I have and previous experience. It's been a long day. I suggest you bed down and be ready for the morning."

"Long day? Hell of a day, more like!"

Hell? You haven't seen even a bit of it yet, Taylor thought.

They spread out across a kilometre wide defence north of the ship that night, with patrols running far and wide to be safe. Taylor sat up against a tree for most of the night, watching the enemy ship. There was not a single light working on it, but the moonlight glinted off the metallic hull. Every half an hour he would look at the site with his night vision equipment just to study it and observe for movement, but there was none.

He heard a branch crack at his side and reacted by reaching for his rifle and twisting around ready to defend himself.

"You should be getting some rest," a calm voice spoke.

He immediately recognised it as Eli, and his shoulders relaxed as he laid the rifle back down over his thighs. She moved up and sat down beside him. He put his arm over her shoulders but could feel little of her through the armour she wore. It didn't matter.

"How much sleep have you had?" she asked.

"Enough."

"I doubt that."

"Did I hear that straight? You're concerned for my health?"

He laughed at the idea even though he felt just the same way about her.

"How much longer do you think this can go on?"

"What?"

"The war, the aliens, when's it all gonna end?"

"Honestly, I'm not sure it ever will."

"What, how can you think that?"

He took in a deep breath, preparing to explain to her the realisation he'd come to in the time of peace they had enjoyed before recent events.

"Look at our own history. Every time one culture has met another, they have fought wars until one is totally defeated or assimilated. There will be no peace between such powers. We aren't strong enough to end them, so they will simply keep coming."

"And they can't seem to take Earth, so what, we just keep fighting?"

Taylor shrugged his shoulders.

"No, I can't believe that. This has to end someday. We keep fighting the way we have, and our luck can't hold forever."

"No," he replied solemnly.

She could see the acceptance in his face for the situation he had just outlined.

"You have accepted it, haven't you? That we're all gonna die?"

"We are all gonna die. We're only human. Only when and where are the questions."

"You know what I mean. We should have years ahead of us."

"And maybe we will. We have made it this far."

"I don't like the way you're talking."

He shrugged his shoulders again.

"I don't want you to throw your life away because you think it's the only way."

"Mmm," he grunted.

With that last sound, the weary Taylor fell asleep with his arm still around Parker. She was deeply dissatisfied with the opinions he had stated, but more than anything she wanted him to rest and recover his full self.

* * *

Taylor awoke to the shouting of Sergeant Major Silva strolling down the lines, drawing the 2nd Inter-Allied from the uneasy sleep they were getting. For many, it was a sharp reminder of the conditions they had faced in France during the first war.

It always amazed Mitch that no matter their location, conditions, or morale, Silva was always the first awake and invigorated, as if powered by some superhuman force. It was exactly the reason he held the position he did, and a reminder that he had chosen the right man.

The air was fresh and clean. The blood and strife of war was behind and in front of them. Now they were stationed in a beautiful land untouched by either war. But it was not to last. He remembered Parker coming to him in the night, but she was nowhere to be seen. He reached for the trunk of the tree he had slept against pulled himself to his feet.

"Damn," he whispered to himself.

It was the best sleep he had gotten since the aliens had come back to their Solar System. He wiped his face and tried to come to his senses. He looked over to the spot where he and Harney had first looked at the enemy positions the night before, just twenty metres along the treeline. Officers of both their units had already gathered, and he could see Jones ensuring they had a sensible representative among them.

Taylor stumbled over towards the officers assembled, and with every step he began to regain his composure until halfway when he finally woke up. He had been fixated on the enemy position for half of the night, and yet slept through the rest like he was back in his own bed.

I wonder if it was a result of Eli being at my side.

When he reached the gathering, he soon realised everything was in hand. He looked to Jones for confirmation. Jones nodded to show things were going to plan.

"Colonel Taylor, I hope you slept well?" Harney asked.

Taylor initially felt a little ashamed to be one of the last officers up, but that feeling quickly receded as he remembered the previous day's events. He turned to look at the enemy crash site in the distance for one last time before joining them. It was still as dead as it was in the night. When he turned back, Jafar was standing there and made him recoil in surprise. He had not heard a sound a second before.

"That ship is empty," he stated.

"Why would you think that?" Taylor asked him.

"Because if they still occupied it, they would be coming at us by now."

Taylor nodded in agreement. It was indeed a strange occurrence for the enemy.

"Walk with me," he said to Jafar.

They continued on to the grouping of officers.

"Colonel, you're gonna want to see this. We have a strike incoming in two minutes," someone shouted.

Why has nobody notified me of this? He first thought, but it didn't matter any longer.

"Looks like we got the best seat in the house," said Harney.

He turned to look on down the valley at the huge vessel. There was still no movement in sight and that made Taylor uncomfortable.

"Why haven't they come at us?"

"Because we have the high ground and numerical superiority," replied Harney.

"No, that would not stop them."

"Then maybe they're just scared."

Taylor smiled.

"No chance. Any sign of our satellite imaging coming back?"

"I've been promised it before noon."

Taylor looked through his binoculars one last time at the tranquil scene. The countryside was beautiful, and there was no sign of the war. The crashed vessel was the only evidence the enemy had been there.

"They've gone. Think about it. Everything up to this point has been to facilitate their retreat back to their main force across the sea."

Harney did not respond, as the possibility would ruin his plan. He checked his watch one last time, and as he did so, he heard the roar of engines approaching rapidly from the north. Before they even had time to look up, missiles were soaring through the sky, and the two aircraft were banking out of sight. Then large missiles hit the hull of the ship and exploded on impact, sending fire and sparks high into the sky. The ship rocked in its position and came to a rest in the same hole it had made for itself.

Troops all along the kilometre line shouted and whistled in joy as they saw black smoke bellow from the enemy ship. There was no doubt it would never fly again. Harney turned to Taylor and stepped up to speak to him personally.

"Whether there were any enemy aboard doesn't matter, but if they were then good. If they weren't, we ensured the ship cannot be repaired, and look what it does for morale."

Taylor could not deny it.

"And if they have run, which I believe they have, it is proof they fear us."

"Do we have any other sightings of enemy in the area?"

"No, in which case you might be right. Our leaders want to buy us time to regroup and gather our strength, which may be exactly what they are doing."

"All the reason we should hit them now."

"That's not for us to decide."

"No, more's the pity."

"Taylor, we got off on the wrong foot, and I am sorry about that. You really saved our asses yesterday, and it won't be forgotten."

"That's my job."

"The 5th are going to continue on south on foot to sweep and clear. I want to be certain none of the alien bastards remain. There must be stragglers about. I want you to perform aerial sweeps of the whole area and destroy any enemy presence you find. I want to hear about any and all enemy sightings and engagements."

"Got it."

Taylor lifted his comms unit.

"Yorath, I need air lift from our the nearest available area north of our position immediately."

"Yes, Sir."

He turned to leave when a new commotion began to his flank.

"Taylor! You need to see this!" Harney called him.

He raced over to the Colonel and his command staff as they laid down a map projector. The device was no bigger than a water bottle but would project a two metres square operations screen for use in the field.

"I've just received reports of massive enemy activity on the Israeli border."

"How big are we talking?"

"We know the wall has been breached. It didn't last

more than twenty minutes. Looks like they're trying to break out from Egypt."

"Why? What is their endgame now?" asked one of Harney's officers.

"They probably realise exactly what we do, that time is on our side. They have to strike hard now, or risk ever-increasing forces as Earth's armies gather. We need to cut off this advance before it can spread. They must be contained," replied Taylor.

"Agreed, and that's exactly what we're going to do."

"What about our task here?" Jones asked.

"A German armoured regiment has already crossed over into the north of the country and are en route to take over here. We have to haul ass. Whatever this enemy advance is, it's moving quick."

He pointed to the map.

"You are to get to the southern outskirts of Hebron immediately. We'll be close behind."

"Looks like a big city."

"Yes, and much of the population has taken up arms and refuses to leave. If the enemy advance reaches the city, the casualties will be substantial."

Taylor lifted his comms unit.

"Inter-Allied assemble immediately, and make your way to the landing zone north of here. Captain Jackson, get your company down here as well, we're moving out fast!"

He gave no information away, but he knew it wasn't

necessary. He and Jones turned and quickly got to a running pace. On both sides he could see their units joining them.

"You wanted to get out there and strike at them. Looks like you got your wish, Mitch!"

"They reached the edge of the treeline, and the three companies swarmed out onto the open plain. The copters swooped in with perfect timing. Taylor barely had to break stride as the ramps of the copters were lowering when they reached them. He rushed aboard to a jovial greeting from Rains as always.

"'Morning, Colonel!"

"You know where we're going?"

"We received our orders from Commander Phillips en route. He's with Captain Jackson now. So we're heading for the holy land?"

"Something like that."

"All aboard!" called Jones.

"Get us in the air, Eddie."

They lifted off after having been on the ground for only a minute.

"Haven't several armies already got forces in the area we're heading?" asked Eddie.

"Yeah, but what is there has taken a beating. Further local troops are on the way with reinforcements coming in from neighbouring countries, but this is big. It's gonna take a lot to hold 'em back."

In just a few short minutes, Italy had gone from view,

and they were over Greece. They could make out the silhouettes of dozens of warships off to their starboard side.

"Why don't we just nuke 'em?"

"I'm sure we'll try soon enough, Eddie, but with the countermeasures we have seen them use before, I doubt it'll work. No, this going to have to be fought with conventional forces, the way we always have."

It was just over an hour when they saw the coastline of Israel. Eddie was about to announce it when they were rocked by an impact, which he only just managed to brush off.

"We got incoming!"

Pulses rushed up between the copters. Taylor grasped one of the handles at the back of the cockpit to brace himself.

"That's coming in from just a little south, maybe around Gaza!" Eddie shouted.

"Christ they must be close!"

A pulse clipped the engine of one of the copters to their side and cut most of its power. They watched as the pilot fought for control but had no hope. The troops inside bailed out and used their boosters to move as far north as they could.

"How much further?" Taylor asked.

"We're coming up on Hebron now!"

"He lifted his Mappad and saw they were over friendly

positions."

"2nd Inter-Allied deploy now, and get these copters to the base north of the city!"

He got to his feet, but as he turned to speak to Eddie, a pulse that ripped a hole in the side of the fuselage struck them. Two of the platoon were thrown out.

"We're going down!"

"Come on!"

Taylor grabbed Eddie and jumped from the door. He knew his boosters would have a hard time breaking the fall of their combined weight over the several hundred metres drop, but it was Rains' only chance of survival.

"I told you that you should have worn your suit!" he yelled at the pilot as they dropped towards the dusty, hard ground."

"I know that now!"

Guns raged below as they could see Israeli armour battling the enemy advance just a few hundred metres south of where they were going to land.

"This is gonna hurt!"

They hit the ground, and Taylor went into a roll, trying to take the impact and cocooned Eddie in the roll. As he tumbled across the ground, he lost his grip, and Rains was tossed out across the dirt. Taylor finally crashed to a halt as his shoulders smashed into a large rock. He groaned in pain, but he could tell he was still in one piece. He rolled over and got up onto one knee to look for Eddie.

"God damn that hurt," he moaned.

He was still flat out on the ground. His clothing was covered in dirt, and his arms were cut and bleeding, but he was alive.

"Next time I say wear your suit, wear you suit!"

"You got no argument from me."

Taylor stumbled over, hauling him to his feet. The others landed all around.

"That could have gone better."

"We're alive aren't we, Charlie?"

He looked up to the line of armour up ahead. To their backs APCs approached, and artillery fire shot overhead from both sides.

"Looks like we landed in the shit," said Eddie. He pulled out his personal sidearm, the only weapon he had on him.

"We need to find you a proper weapon."

"I'm sure there'll be no shortage lying about the ground."

Taylor motioned for them to go forward even though they were still missing several platoons. He got to a jogging pace as he could see the tanks were fighting from a crest that hid the enemy from view. As they neared, he slowed and through the dust and smoke could see that troops were scattered along the edge and lying in prone positions.

"Friendlies coming in!" he yelled.

There was so much fire all around that only a handful of the soldiers even noticed. He ducked down and went prone beside a few that had turned to acknowledge them. For a moment, they looked both surprised and confused to see their uniforms, but within seconds they no longer cared.

"Colonel Taylor, who's your commanding officer?"

"He's dead. Lieutenant Amar is in charge. She's over there!" he shouted, pointing east along the line."

"Thanks." He noticed several of Jones' platoon had started taking shots at the enemy who were still two hundred metres out.

"Ota! Jackson! Take up position here. Grey spread out to the west! Jones you're with me!"

He got up and rushed behind the cover of the nearest tank while he looked out east. He could see a women shouting at several of the troops and guessed it was Amar. Dead IDF soldiers lay around her position, and a medic was fighting to save one of the wounded. He rushed over to her position and hit the dirt beside her. His landing threw dust up over the Lieutenant. She spat it out, looking back at Taylor ready to yell at him but saw he wasn't one of hers.

"Colonel Taylor, we're here to help."

"About time!"

"What can we do?"

"Get firing. We've got thousands of Mechs advancing on us. We've lost five kilometres in the last hour. Much further and we'll be at the city!"

He looked back to Jones and his company and beckoned for them to move forward and take the positions where the dead lay. They were almost shoulder-to-shoulder with the IDF soldiers wedged between two tanks, one of which was a burning wreck. Taylor put his rifle on the shelf they were using for cover and immediately targeted the first Mech. They were advancing in waves and quickly covering the ground. Several armoured vehicles from both sides lay burning across the plain.

There were so many targets to choose from, he could almost fire blind and still hit something. The enemy front expanded as far as he could see both sides, though smoke and dust limited visibility. Pulses exploded all around, and he felt the burning residue landing everywhere. A heavy weapon beyond his sight hit the surviving tank next to them. The turret was ripped from the hull and sent hurtling twenty metres behind them. He looked back to the enemy and could see a never-ending surge of Mechs and armoured vehicles.

Taylor turned to look at what they had at their backs, and there was nothing but empty space. He grabbed Amar's arm, forcing her to turn away from the battle.

"We can't stay here!" he shouted at her.

"We have to. There is only a kilometre left between here and the city."

"Then we will have to take up position in the city outskirts."

"I won't leave my post!"

Without thinking, he slapped her hard across the face. He hated himself for doing it, but he didn't see a woman before him; he saw a brave officer who was going to be dead, along with all her comrades if he didn't act. Blood seeped from her mouth, and she said nothing.

"This position has fallen. Don't be foolish and stay here to die. Fall back, regroup, and stay in this fight."

It was the reality check she needed, even if it did hurt her pride more than her jaw. She spoke something in Hebrew through her comms unit that meant nothing to Taylor, and then shouted a second time louder. She staggered to get to her feet. She was clearly exhausted. Taylor reached out and helped her.

"Fallback!" he ordered.

He repeated the same into his radio. He turned to see Eddie taking a rifle from one of the bodies and salvaging what ammunition he could. Taylor knew how heavy the bulky weapons were without the aid of a suit and did not envy him for having to manage it.

They got to a quick jogging pace as a few of the tanks began to roll back with them. Taylor could see that less than half of the Israeli armour at the line was able to move.

"We're losing a lot of ground!" said Amar.

"And we'll lose a lot more until we get some serious support," replied Taylor.

"We were promised support from all over, but you're the first to arrive."

"We have another regiment en route. Should be here within an hour."

"Then I hope we can last that long. Militias have made defences at the edge of the city. We'll have to hold there."

The Israelis were one of the few nations still putting people through National Service, and he knew that meant they'd at least have some training, though he doubted their equipment would be up to muster. Pulses still burst around them from indirect fire. The shelf they had fought from at least covered their retreat. Jafar rushed up beside Taylor. He didn't seem to shock Amar. It seemed news of one of the enemy fighting alongside the humans was spreading quickly now.

A few minutes later, they had passed behind the range of the enemy guns and thought they'd reached safety, but it was not to be. Aircraft rushed overhead, and a new wave of enemy pulses crashed down in between them as they ran for their lives. Soldiers from both units were thrown through the air by blasts and tossed around like rag dolls.

One of the pulses burst in front of Taylor, and he dipped his head just in time for the shrapnel to brush over his helmet and save his face. The crater left in front of him was four metres wide and a metre deep.

"They're not going to let up, are they?" asked Jones.

"No," replied Jafar.

"At this rate, they'll be in Jerusalem by tomorrow unless we can stop them," said Amar.

They kept running, and it wasn't long before they could see the defensive positions at the edge of the city. Several kilometres of trench works and walls were being manned by the militias. The defences were at least a welcome sight. They reached the trenches and flooded inside. The pulses continued to burst all around them. Amar and Taylor stuck together as they slid into a trench. The militia looked scared. Taylor could already see they were beginning to regret standing their ground once they could see the troops running for their lives.

"Jones, get on to Phillips and find out when we're getting reinforced!"

"Nobody has seen the Commander since hitting the ground. Word is his copter was hit on the way in."

"Well, find a radio and get on to Harney, and tell him we need more than just 5th Marine Regiment!"

"I'll do what I can."

We're in deep shit, Taylor thought.

The bombardment settled down a few minutes later, but they knew it wouldn't last.

"Be nice if we had some aerial support."

"We did this morning. They took a beating," replied Amar.

"Let's get this straight. We can't stop them. If we don't get some serious numbers here soon, we're gonna be swept back to Jerusalem in no time."

It was too late. The enemy was already at the edge of the city with their rapid blitz to cut a path through human lines. The tanks begun firing, but the enemy was still out of range of their rifles.

We can't have made it this far to die in the dirt here.

"Ready your weapons and hold fast!" he yelled.

Jones came running down the line, and he prayed it was good news.

"What is it?"

"Harney has been ordered to the defence of Jerusalem. All forces are ordered to rally there."

He looked over to Amar.

"That goes for you too, Lieutenant. This is a joint command for all allied forces in the area."

"What about all these people? We can't leave them."

"No, but neither I am willing to risk my life and the lives or my people because they're too stubborn to save their own skins. Tell them they'll all die if they stay, and that they need to move out immediately. If they go now, we'll stay and defend these trenches for ten minutes to give them a head start."

She knew it was the best offer she was going to get, and she wasn't keen to stay and die either.

"Time is running short, Lieutenant."

She nodded in agreement and turned away to relay the message for her soldiers to convey along the border of the city.

"Ten minutes for them to get through town?"

"It's ten minutes longer than I want to stay here, Jones."

"True, but what about us? We'll have a hell of a time getting through with all them ahead of us?"

"After their ten minutes is up, they're on their own. I want us air lifted out of here."

"Now we're talking!" yelled Eddie.

"Find us somewhere they can pick us up and radio it in," Taylor said to Jones.

Amar stepped back up to his side.

"Looks like most of them are excepting it and moving on."

"Well they better. It ain't much of a window to get clear. We're getting airlifted out of here as soon as those ten minutes are up. I suggest you do the same."

"No, we'll fight a retreat back to Jerusalem to make sure the civilians make it."

Taylor nodded in agreement. He knew it was going to cost them lives, but he was done arguing.

"They should have gotten these people out hours ago," Jones whispered.

"Yep, and there's only so much we can do for them. We have a duty to our fellow marines, and I intend to honour it."

The civilians were climbing out of the trenches as the enemy reached the effective distance of their rifles. Taylor didn't have to give the order to fire. They all knew what to do, and the sharpshooters among them carefully took the first few shots. Thirty seconds later, the Battalion opened up with everything it had. The thousands of Mechs bearing down on their position were a frightening sight even to the combat hardened veterans.

The enemy fell one rank after the other, but a never-ending stream poured over the bodies. Taylor could see their numbers were expanding to the flanks. The civilians had gotten just five minutes lead-time when the enemy reached the onehundred metre mark. Explosions erupted all along the line, but they suffered few casualties due to their deep trenches. The enemy artillery fire intensified in the last three minutes.

Despite the continuous fire they put down, they seemed to have little effect on the enemy advance, and the increasing amount of fire was forcing them to keep their heads down.

"That's enough!"

"It's only been eight minutes!" replied Jones.

"Fuck it, they brought this on themselves by being such idiots." He lifted his intercom as an explosion sent dirt and stones smashing into his helmet, forcing the two officers to duck down.

"Fall back! Fall back now!"

They clambered out of the trenches under a hail of gunfire. Jones covered Taylor's back with his shield, saving him from one of the pulses before he'd got a metre from the trench. Mitch still hadn't found a replacement since his was destroyed the day before, a fact he was all too aware off as the shards of the pulse burst over Jones' shield and flew past his head.

He turned back briefly to check if his unit were following him. There was nothing left to say or do but run. The speed their suits allowed them was more welcome than ever as explosions erupted all around. At a sprinting pace, they reached the nearest buildings in less than a minute and passed on from line of sight with the enemy.

Taylor lifted his Mappad, checking the location the copters had been requested for, but he didn't slow his pace any.

Please, please be there, he thought.

They took a bend up ahead where it opened up into a soccer field. Jones had chosen the location well. The birds were waiting for them.

"hallefuckinglujah!" yelled Rains.

Taylor turned to see the pilot was at the front, and he was wearing one of the Reitech suits. He had no idea where he had pillaged it from, but he didn't care. Whoever he got it from no longer needed it. He came to a halt and ushered his people through, to be certain all the survivors were there. They had taken minor casualties, considering the mass of forces that had assaulted them.

The last few ran past him, and he gladly took to his

feet, rushing for Jones who was waiting at the door to one of the copters for him. He breathed a sigh of relief as he stepped up into the craft.

"All of that for what, saving some idiots who wouldn't leave when they should have?"

"They're people's homes, Charlie. Would you be so eager to leave yours?"

"If I knew this was coming, hell yes!"

Taylor pulled the door shut behind him and was glad the onslaught was over.

"Let's get these birds in the air!"

CHAPTER NINE

From the second they put down at the defensive line at Jerusalem, Taylor knew it was like nothing he had seen before. Multiple nations of often-conflicting religions had gathered to defend the city in unprecedented numbers. Deep trenches had been dug for hundreds of kilometres. Behind them lay thick concrete walls with gun emplacements every twenty metres and tanks having to sit almost track to track in some places.

He stepped off the copter to a wholly different world to anything he had experienced in the second war for Earth. Jones stopped and took a deep breath and exhaled.

"Ahh, that's gotta make you feel good."

"What?" Taylor asked.

"The smell of oil, grease, fresh dirt, liquid concrete, and sweat. All the things that we need."

"Maybe for you. A good night's sleep and the company

of a fine woman is more what I had in mind," Taylor joked.

Jones smiled, for he knew Taylor revelled in it as much as he did.

"If we can't hold this, we can't hold shit."

"Eloquently put," Jones replied.

"About as eloquent as your love of grease and sweat, you limey bastard," he laughed.

It was good to be back among allies and the safety of strong defences. The rapport had completely changed in the initial moments that the stress had been taken off them.

"They chose the wrong city to go for," added Jones. "Too many people will fight to the bitter end for this one."

"And maybe that is why they chose it. Maybe capturing it would have significant impact on the belief which humanity has, that it can win."

"I don't doubt it would, but they can't take it anyhow."

"Not now we're here."

"Mmm," mumbled Jones as he looked across the endless lines of allied troops and armour. It was a comforting setting, which would have been a welcome thing through much of their experiences.

He knelt down to the brew of tea he had going on a stove he had managed to acquire quickly upon their arrival. Taylor leant against the edge of the rampart wall to look at the dust cloud to the south. It was the massive enemy army approaching.

"Want one?" asked Jones.

Taylor pulled out of his empty canteen and separated the base, passing it to his friend. They both knew it was the last moment of peace they would see for some time.

"That looks like ours," said Taylor.

Jones left his brew and stood up to see what he meant. Taylor lifted his binoculars.

"Son of a bitch. It's Phillips. He made it."

The Commander had an arm over a soldier each side of him, and a leg wound clearly having been patched up.

"Should we go to him?"

"No, that wound has earned him a pass out of this fight. There'll be time enough to reunite if we make it through."

They watched as the Commander was hauled through one of the main gates a few hundred metres east of their position. Jones was quick to get back to his brew and handed Taylor his canteen.

"How many soldiers do you believe we have here, Mitch?"

"I can tell you how many marines we have here, that's for sure."

"You know what I mean."

"Who knows? Must be tens of thousands spread over hundred of kilometres. They say the line extends from Tel Aviv to the Dead Sea. Could even be hundreds of thousands with those still arriving."

"Colonel Taylor!"

He turned to see Harney approaching along the wall.

"Good to see your boys made it."

"Very nearly didn't. That was a total fuck up at Hebron."

"Maybe, but every action further south has bought us time to get as much here as humanly possible."

He looked past Taylor's shoulder to address Jafar. He had been sitting quietly on the edge of the wall for some time.

"Do you think it will be enough, Sergeant?"

"If everyone here stands his ground, yes."

"That's what I like, a solid answer. We're positioned east of here, past the next tower. I just saw Commander Phillips go through the gates. Good to see him alive, but he'll be sitting this one out."

"Who is in charge here?" asked Taylor.

"Honestly, nobody knows. There are high-ranking officers from six or seven armies amongst us. Communications aren't centrally managed, so right now, it seems each force is in charge of their own lump of turf. I'll have my hands full with the 5th. I suggest you handle your own shit as well."

He nodded in agreement.

Great, nobody breathing down our neck and trying to get us killed.

The Colonel turned to look out south towards Hebron. They could now just make out the silhouettes of the enemy heavy tanks across the barren landscape. They were surrounded by swarms of what were clearly Mechs but still several kilometres out.

"I'll leave you to it, Taylor, good luck."

"And to you, Colonel," he replied.

Harney strode off along the line to return to his regiment.

"A whole regiment? As a Colonel, you should have the same," said Jones.

"Yeah, but you know how it is. It's easy to promote individual officers, not so easy to recruit, train, and sustain a full regiment. Anyway, I can't say I'd be interested. This Battalion is a handful as it is. I liked commanding a company. It was tight and flexible. It worked."

"And this still works now!"

It was a reminder to both of them that the real missing link was Chandra.

"Well it sure is nice to have numbers on our side, anyway," added Jones to lighten the tone.

A loud boom rang out as one of the heavy gun emplacements fired the first shot.

"It's begun, Charlie."

He leaned in against the wall with his canteen of tea still steaming. He never understood how a hot drink could be so soothing even in a hot climate, but he knew now why Jones was always so keen to brew up. The shell from the gun landed just shy of the enemy vehicle it targeted, but another soared out from the gun within a few seconds of the shot landing.

It was almost deafening. The turret looked more like it had come off a warship than anything else. It was far larger than anything their tanks used.

"I guess they had the defence of this city in mind for a while!" shouted Jones.

"They must have fought here in the first war. Question is, did the area hold because they built these defences, or did they build them when they recovered the ground?"

Neither of them knew for sure what had happened through much of the Middle East in the first war. It was such a far away land for them at the time, it seemed of little concern. For the next hour, they watched the enemy attempt to advance across the open terrain. Their tanks slugged it out with the gun emplacements and tank regiments of several countries who had sent aid. There was little for those on the walls to do but hunker down and avoid the fire until they closed the distance.

After a few minutes of watching the battle, Taylor and Jones sat down against the barricades and propped their rifles up beside them, resting their weary legs. It was a strange experience for them, to be able to rest while the battle raged all around them. So often they had been the frontline in battles, and now they were several lines back from it. They didn't envy those down in the trenches before them. The thick concrete and steel walls that were five metres high provided a solid defence against all but the heaviest weapons.

The hour passed before the infantry below began to engage the enemy with anti-tank weapons and small arms soon after. They knew it meant the aliens were just a hundred or so metres out of their range. Taylor finally got to his feet, and it was a welcome break after sitting on hard concrete for so long. He looked to the east and west. It was much the same sight as was in front of them. Lines of burning tanks were being used as cover from the enemy advance, and thick smoke and dust made the battle seem so much smaller than he knew it to be.

"They're slowing down," said Jones.

"Yeah, can you blame them? Look at the beating they're taking."

"You think this means we have stopped them?"

Taylor looked to Jafar.

"They cannot keep this up for much longer. It would be foolish."

"No, coming back to Earth was foolish. It was the biggest mistake they ever made," Taylor replied.

"It's not over yet," added Charlie.

"2nd Inter-Allied, fire in your own time once in range," Taylor ordered across their comms.

It was clear to him that if the enemy did reach their range, there wouldn't be much fight left in them. Despite that, they continued to drive forward. But he could see the back of their ranks now. No longer were they an endless column of armour and soldiers. They were spreading thin across the plain.

"They're thinning out."

"Or they've held back the next waves," replied Jones.

"Either way, this is the turning point."

He lifted his rifle onto the rampart and could see they were so close now to being within range. His finger wrapped around the trigger as he took aim at the Mech who was going to enter his sights first. Just another few metres and he could fire, but the creature was killed by a burst from the soldiers below. He was about to swear at the pleasure of the kill being taken from him, but he knew there would be so many more opportunities.

"Almost there!" yelled Jones.

A huge mass of Mechs took to a running pace, trying to rush for the trench positions. It brought them immediately into range. Taylor smiled as he shouted.

"Fire!"

He had already given them the 'fire at will' command, but he could not resist crying out. Volley upon volley poured from the walls into the Mech advance. It was a new layer of defences the enemy had not yet encountered, and it was devastating. In just three minutes, their lines were crippled, and they began to falter.

"Go on, run you bastards!" Jones screamed.

Just as he shouted it, many did turn and run. Cries of

excitement rang out from the trenches below, followed by shouts that seemingly called for an advance. Hundreds of IDF troops then climbed out of their trenches and rushed forward to pursue the fleeing enemy.

"No! Stay in the trenches!"

None of them heard Taylor over the distance and noise.

"What the hell are they doing?"

They watched as the success overcame the troops, causing them to forget the dangers posed by the enemy. Screams rang from all around them, and they could tell a similar practice was taking place along the line. Taylor could do nothing but stand and watch.

"Idiots."

"Dead idiots," Jones added.

The enemy had retreated a kilometre from the wall when they stopped and stood their ground. From that distance, they could just make out the lines of pulses smashing into troops who had given pursuit. They watched silently as they were slaughtered in the open ground and joined the mounds of enemy dead.

"What a waste," said Jones.

It was a sign of things to come. The day passed with occasional barrages from the larger guns, but no movement from either side. Taylor and his troops slept on the wall that night. There hadn't been any suggestion of billets for them, and there seemed nobody keen to replace them. A supply of ration packs handed out in the evening was the only luxury they enjoyed.

Taylor slept well that night. The great defences provided some comfort and sense of security. He was so exhausted that he doubted he could have stayed awake even if he'd wanted to. He had seen no need to set watches. The platoon commanders were already on it themselves.

An hour after first light, the sun lifted the temperature at a rapid rate, enough to wake Taylor from his deep sleep. The shining rays of sunlight blurred his vision and stunned him slightly as he got up. As he propped himself against the wall, Jones thrust an almost fresh cup of tea into his hands. He took it gladly but still wished it were coffee.

"Thanks."

It was surprisingly quiet, almost eerily so. Only a few footsteps broke the silence. His eyes began to adjust, and he peered out to the south as he took a sip. The bodies from the trenches had been cleared, and fresh troops now occupied them. The barren space from then onwards was still littered with bodies though. He cast his gaze across to the enemy side to see they too had dug in. Trench works largely hid their numbers, and he could see for kilometres each side now that the enemy positions extended as far as the eye could see.

"They're using trenches," stated Jafar.

Taylor turned in surprise to see the alien wide-awake and standing at his side.

"What of it?"

"I told you this. When they begin to dig in, it is because their tactics are failing. The Krycenaean armies never stop attacking unless they cannot succeed."

"So they are beaten?"

"For now. Until they can reinforce or find a different way to breach this line."

"Why don't they go round us?" asked Jones.

Taylor grunted in agreement.

"Yeah, they have ships, so why fight us in open combat?"

"Because it is their way, and if they cannot beat us in open combat, it is failure for them."

"So we just slug it out here until one side is done for?" asked Jones.

"Yes."

"Well, I don't know about you, but I'd like to see this ended sooner rather than later. Another army could come through that Gateway anytime and reinforce these bastards."

"Not likely."

"No? And why is that, Jafar?"

"Because Demiran has committed everything he has, and none of the other Lords would want to help him succeed."

"But they all want Earth, do they not?"

"Yes, but if Demiran wins, even with the support of another Lord, he will claim the planet his own."

Taylor laughed.

"What is so funny?" asked Jafar.

"These Lords, if they'd rallied together, they could have ended us all years ago."

Jafar shrugged his shoulders.

"So, through their own vanity and individual desire for power, they'd see nobody succeed rather than share a success? That's fucking brilliant," replied Charlie.

"I have to say I'm glad to hear it. Otherwise, we'd be in deep shit," added Taylor.

"And what if one day these Lords manage some kind of joint military pact? We'd be annihilated."

"Then pray they don't, Jones."

The enemy artillery and tanks opened fire with a fresh barrage, forcing them to duck down for cover. Taylor watched through the gaps in the rampart. The enemy was again advancing towards their walls.

"It's a God damn siege," he whispered to himself.

Their guns began to return fire, and everyone knew the next attack was coming. Within two hours of the sun rising, the enemy were once more being broken at their defensive line, but the casualties were mounting on both sides. Just as it appeared they would end the attack, as they had the previous day on Earth, a shattering explosion erupted to the west. The walls shook in their foundations and rumbled beneath their feet.

Huge chunks of metal and concrete were thrown into the air, and smaller debris even managed to reach Taylor and the others. It showered down on their helmets, forcing them to look away for a moment. When they recovered, they could see the wall had been breached. Taylor turned back to see the enemy forces were funnelling from each side in towards the hole in the perimeter. Gunfire smashed into their flanks, but it was not enough to stop them reaching the weak point. The troops in the trenches before the breach were quickly overwhelmed and driven aside.

Thousands of Mechs were pushing forwards to the breach with many more crossing no man's land to seize the opportunity.

"What do we do?" asked Jones.

"We have to go."

Taylor strolled to the inner edge of the deep walls and looked down to see a mass of troops sitting around with nothing to do. He didn't recognise their uniforms, but they were well equipped and available. He pinpointed the nearest officer and shouted at him.

"You there!"

The officer clearly heard him and froze.

"Get these men up onto the wall. There has been a breach which we have to deal with!"

The man was still frozen for a second. Taylor could not work out if he was just surprised, or if he didn't understand English. He pointed down to the group of troops and gestured for them to get up onto the walls.

"Get them up here now!"

He lifted his comms device.

"We have a breach to the west. Replacements will fill our positions. Inter-Allied follow me!"

He turned to check those around him were ready, grabbed his rifle, and leapt from the wall. He used his suit's boosters to launch him down into the nearest opening, and then immediately jumped clear of a line of instant shelters, landing not far from where troops were rushing to fill the breach. He was surprised they could barely see through to the hole in the wall for the mass of soldiers and tanks moving up to defend it.

Taylor looked up to the top of the wall to see the breach was twenty metres wide, and the walls either side had been cleared by the debris. Nobody remained on the stretch of ramparts.

"Up onto the wall!" he shouted into his comm.

They used their boosters twice more to land accurately onto the defensive positions. He knew it was about all the power they had, but if they couldn't hold the wall, it wouldn't matter anyway. He landed first on the walls and found a dozen dead soldiers scattered across the battlement, most of them killed by the explosion and shrapnel from it.

He reached the edge where the wall had fallen just as the rest of the Inter-Allied force landed around him, either side of the breach. They filled the wall from one tower to the next, replacing those who had been killed and thrown from the position. He drew both grenades he had left and threw them into the mass of enemy Mechs advancing between the gap. Fire was rained down on the attackers from both sides, and he could see the brutal onslaught lashed on those defending from inside the walls.

A few pulses raced past their heads, but they were firing from relative safety on the wall that had stayed firm, despite the massive blast. After fifteen minutes, the bodies of the Mechs were beginning to pile up, to the extent that others were struggling to make their way through. Taylor was reaching for his last magazine, and knew the others would be in a similar position, when they began to turn and flee.

He looked back at their allies, seeing they had learned from their last experience. They fought the enemy up to the breach and stopped. No one wanted to throw their lives away. He turned back to the battlefield and took a few more carefully aimed shots until the magazine was empty. He was shooting the enemy in the back as they fled, but he felt no sympathy for them. Jafar was doing the same beside him.

All along the walls, troops were shouting and whistling. He could not distinguish one voice from another and suspected it was a mix of insults and celebrations. He could see they had taken few casualties along the edge of the wall.

"We couldn't have managed much longer than that.

Ammo was running thin."

"Tell me about it," he replied.

"Still, two waves repulsed. That must mean something, Jafar."

"It does. It means we have ground them to a halt."

He rested up against the wall and watched joyfully as the enemy fell back to their positions.

"Send for ammo. We're gonna need a lot more."

The excitement of their victory soon died down as the troops along the kilometres of defences lay about to await the enemy's next move. The day passed into night without any more than a couple of exchanges between the artillery. The troops who had survived the trenches had worked to strengthen their positions all day.

When morning came, Taylor looked down from the wall and was surprised to see Commander Phillips approaching with a crutch under one arm and his other arm in a sling. One of his eyes was swollen and cuts showed beneath it. He looked like he'd been through hell. Phillips looked out at the mound of enemy bodies still lying in the breach only metres from where Taylor had slept. The troops had begun to clear the bodies but barely made a dent in their number.

"'Morning, Sir!"

Phillips balanced on his crutch and held up his good arm, trying to block the sunlight silhouetting Taylor's figure against the sky. Taylor could see him struggling to see so jumped down onto the nearest ramp to approach the Commander.

"Good to see you made it, Sir."

"Likewise, Colonel. And you held here. I'm impressed."

Taylor looked surprised.

"You doubted we could do it?"

"If you'd asked me a week ago, I wouldn't have doubted your chances of anything, but after we got hit on the way in, and seeing what was on the ground, I thought we were done for. It was only because I was carried out that I am here now."

"And back on your feet."

"Just about."

"You'll be back in the fight in no time."

"Not quite, Colonel. Our job here is done."

"How so?"

"Local forces are taking over, now that they have halted the enemy advance. The Battalion is to return to Naples for some R&R, followed by preparation for the next operation."

Taylor smiled and was utterly relieved, which took Phillips by surprise.

"You're happy about this? I thought you'd be pissed that someone else would be stepping in after you'd done the hard work."

"Hell, no, you think I like fighting those bastards? We're good to go."

Phillips smiled back in return, wincing in pain.

"They got you some pain meds?"

"Basic stuff yeah, anything stronger, and I won't be fit to command. Get the Battalion up and moving to the coordinates that are being sent to your Mappad presently. It's a few clicks north of here, and there aren't any vehicles spare."

"We don't mind walking."

In truth, he did in the sweltering heat, but not so much when it was to return to a safe and relaxing environment where he could kick back for a while.

"Are we waiting to be relieved?"

"No, there are more than enough troops here to fill your place. Get moving now."

He passed on the order through his comms, and within seconds, the troops were clambering down the ramps. They didn't know yet where they were heading, but it seemed unfair to their allies to celebrate the end of the fight for them when the enemy wasstill very much at their door. Jones was first down from the defences and as surprised to see Phillips as Taylor was.

"On your feet already, Sir?" he asked.

"Near enough. I'll be hitching a ride to join you presently. One of the Generals has kindly offered his personal vehicle to get me there. I don't think I'll be walking any distance for some time."

He hobbled aside as the troops began to back up

behind Taylor and waved for them to pass. Taylor led the way through the encampment. They hadn't travelled north beyond the wall before, and only seen it from their position. Line after line of trenches had been dug to give some shelter from the aerial and artillery bombardments. Armour had been dug into hull-up positions in multiple tiered defences spanning two kilometres north.

"You think we really did it, stopped them?" asked Jones.

"Looks that way. They aren't getting anywhere coming this way."

"They could just go east."

"No," replied Jafar. "They will want to prove they can win here."

"Then that'll be their undoing."

"So where we heading?"

"Back to Italy, Charlie, rest up and prepare for the eventual counteroffensive."

"You're bullshitting us, right?"

Taylor shook his head.

"Thank God for that. Let some other bastards to the hard work for once."

"We were only called in as an emergency measure, after all."

"Yeah, and that usually entails us up to our necks in shit for a year."

"Well, it ain't over yet."

"Come on, Mitch, enjoy what we're getting."

"Mmm," he mumbled.

They continued walking past the lines of armour, and he knew everyone in the Battalion would be curious to know where they were going, though he suspected those who had eavesdropped on their conversation would have spread the rumours like wild fire along the column.

"What'll happen here now, do you think?"

"Meat grinder, Charlie. If Jafar is right, and they keep throwing themselves at the defenders, and those defenders are unwilling to give up the city, it could go on for some time. The casualties will be horrific. They have to be."

"Could buy us some time though."

"Yep, that's what General White was talking about. Gather our forces before we hit them and finish 'em for good."

"I bet there's more than a few who think now we've stopped them, we should just leave them there."

"No doubt, luckily those idiots aren't in charge. Last time we thought we could just let 'em be, we paid a dear price. We should have continued under wartime conditions this time last year. At least the Navy construction did."

"Yep, saved our arses."

"But the idea this battle could have been won in space was foolish. They were always coming for Earth."

Jones turned to Jafar.

"You really believe if we can destroy Demiran and this army he has here that Earth will be safe?"

"Not safe, but safe from an invasion force."

"What else could we have to fear?"

"Demiran has always fought with only brute strength, the same as his kin, Karadag. But the other Lords should not be underestimated."

"We just maintain strong forces here, and we'll be fine," replied Taylor.

"If we crush this army, what's stopping us going back to Tau Ceti and crushing the rest of these Lords?" asked Jones.

Taylor shook his head as he thought about their first expedition to the enemy system.

"Didn't we lose enough the first time around?"

"And that is a reason not to try?"

"Demiran's armies were the most powerful, but threatening their homeworlds you could force the Lords to unite."

"Just like our armies have here," added Jones.

"Then why did we ever go there in the first place?"

"I warned you all of the dangers of Tau Ceti."

Taylor nodded and remembered.

"Let's just enjoy what we do have. Let's crush this Demiran scumbag and his armies, and then we may just stand a chance of living in peace."

"And that is what you want?"

Taylor seemed surprised at Jafar's question.

"What else would I want?"

"You are a fighter, one of the best. Why stop doing what you are so good at?"

"We fight because we have to, not because we like to."

Taylor could see it was a concept that was still taking time to settle in with his alien friend. Tsengal and Jafar seemed to do nothing but train in the time between the wars.

"Back when you served Demiran, what did you do when there was no war to fight?" asked Jones.

"We protected Demiran and trained to be better fighters."

"And the idea of being able to rest, relax, and do your own thing never appealed to you?"

"It was never an option I could ever have thought of."

CHAPTER TEN

Taylor was glad to see Gallo waiting for them when they landed at the Major's base. A broad grin span across his face, and he had organised a welcoming party for the Battalion, including the Mayor of Naples. Taylor would have welcomed a rest, but appreciated the effort that had been made. He stepped out first from the copter to a round of applause from the several hundred-strong crowd, waving Italian, American, and British flags at them.

"This is Mayor Manciolino of Napoli."

Taylor shook his hand and put on a smile, but he felt more than a little awkward. They had secured victory over the enemy, for now.

"It is an honour to have such a distinguished officer here, thank you," said the Mayor.

Taylor nodded and couldn't think of anything to say.

"You must be hungry. The Mayor has prepared a meal

for you and your troops here this evening."

That's the first good thing I've heard, he thought.

He couldn't see any way of continuing on. The crowd blocked them in against the copters.

"Mayor, your welcome is much appreciated, but you must excuse us. The men and women of this Battalion have fought hard and lost friends. What they need right now is some peace and quiet to recover. My apologies."

"No, Colonel, my apologies for keeping you. We welcome you back to our city and look forward to seeing you all this evening."

He turned around and shouted with a booming voice for the crowd to clear. They parted in seconds and let the troops through. Gallo leapt to Taylor's side to walk with him.

"Good to see you made it."

"Thanks, have you had any enemy contact since we've been gone?"

"Little, a couple of encounters. Colonel Harney left a company here to deal with them."

"So did you see any action?"

"I saw the enemy, called it in, and the Colonel's marines dealt with it."

Taylor could hear the sound of disappointment in his voice.

"Trust me, you didn't miss anything. Your time will come to face those things, and you won't long for it a second time."

He could see Gallo didn't believe him, but there was only one way to convince him otherwise, and that would be the hard way.

"How many did you kill?" asked Gallo.

"I don't know, not enough."

"You are here to help train us now. We couldn't hope for better mentors."

"Really? Are those our orders?" he asked.

"I believe so. We have been told to expect this equipment you use by the end of the week, and we are to follow a training regime as organised by yourself to see we are fit for combat."

"Mmm," Taylor muttered.

He'd looked forward to taking it easy for a while, not training near raw recruits, but it was hard to put down the Major who spoke with such fire and enthusiasm.

"You must need time to prepare for the grand meal which has been planned for you."

The idea of scrubbing up and having to look presentable for the Mayor doesn't seem all that rewarding for the work we've done, but who am I to refuse?

"We'll be there, Major."

Gallo responded with a smile before splitting off a happy spring in his feet.

"God save us," whispered Taylor sarcastically.

They reached their billets to find they were exactly as

they had left them, though beyond their positions more accommodation had been assembled for whoever was to join them. Jones strode up to him.

"All this talk of amassing forces for a big push over the water. I only hope they understand quite what it will take to make any headway, and not get driven back into the sea."

"I think the World leaders will understand after they see what is going on at Jerusalem. We'll need hundreds of thousands of soldiers to win this war, let alone all the logistics and support staff that goes with it."

"Support staff, fucking MPs then."

"Inevitably."

"That's all we bloody need."

"A necessary evil."

"Sometimes, and just sons of bitches the rest."

Taylor had to laugh.

* * *

A grand marquee had been assembled for their evening celebration, and it was lit up as the sun went down. Taylor stepped out of his billet wearing a clean set of BDUs. It was a long way from appropriate for such a function, but the best he could muster. Parker joined him andthey walked towards the festivities.

"Feels good, doesn't it, to be able to enjoy an evening

once more? You take it for granted until war comes around again," she said.

"Can't say I'm having much fun yet."

"You will."

He turned to see she was utterly confident of the fact, and that did boost his spirits a little. They walked hand in hand through the darkness until they came into the floodlights of the marquee and quickly let go.

Guards from Gallo's unit stood at the entrance in their finest uniforms. They looked more like model soldiers than real ones, which he knew they pretty much were. They saluted across their chests with rifles held on the other arms. He was being given an excessive amount of attention and respect that was starting to bore him, but Mitch couldn't see anyway to stop it.

As he entered the marquee, the music stopped, and the Mayor introduced him. He could tell the man had already drunk a good amount before the food had been served.

"Welcome to the brave Colonel Taylor! It is an honour for him to be with us this evening!"

Taylor waved off the Mayor and continued onwards to more familiar faces. The officers of Inter-Allied shared a table, and that meant leaving Parker at the door to find her own way. It saddened him to leave her on their night of celebrations, but he knew they had to maintain the divide between officers and the rest. It was a fact Jones was all to keen to remind him of.

"Come on, Mitch, join the exclusive club!"

He could already tell Jones had been necking wine for the last hour or more.

Wine? I'd kill for a beer.

As he approached, Charlie held out a glass of red for him. With the heat of the country and thick air, he wanted nothing more than something chilled, but he knew it had all been provided for them. He took the glass and turned to the Mayor, lifting his glass in gratitude.

Taylor knocked back a mouthful of the wine, and despite it being an ambient temperature red, it went down smoother than expected. It was soothing and warm, which was somehow comforting and relaxing despite the heat of the day.

"Just wait till the port comes!" yelled Charlie.

"Port?" asked Eddie. You decadent bastard!" he laughed.

Jones smiled and fully embraced the decadent nature of it.

He took a seat at the table and noticed the smell of the food being brought to the tables. It was fresh and oozing in flavour. They had returned to wartime conditions so quickly, but it had been a stark reminder of what they now had to endure. The prospect of a real meal was an immensely appealing idea even after a few days of MREs.

"Ahh, pasta!"

He knew exactly what Charlie meant and was starting

to appreciate the occasion. In just fifteen minutes of good food and drink in a warm friendly environment, he began to see the lighter side of things and indulge a little. Halfway through the evening, the Mayor called for silence and stood up to address the people present.

His face was pinkish red and sweaty from the large volumes of wine and laughter. He wobbled slightly as he stood. That got a few laughs from the troops, which he also seemed to find funny. He started speaking to them in Italian but stopped himself halfway through his second sentence, realising their guests had no clue as to what he was saying.

"On behalf of our city, and our country, I wish to thank Colonel Taylor and the 2nd Inter-Allied. They have fought for many years for our safety and lands. For which ever country they fought in, whichever continent and even in space, they fought for us all."

Gallo was the first on his feet to clap and cheer. But speaking of the previous war was a reminder of how much work was to come, and how much more blood would spill. Many of the other Italians joined in the applause, but Taylor's people managed little more than a lazy clap. Manciolino called for quiet and could barely get any more words out, as he scoffed down half a glass of wine and held the other half up to a toast.

"To our friends and allies!"

It gained a round of applause but most were more

interested in knocking back their drinks. He finally slumped back down to his seat.

"We're going to feel this in the morning," said Taylor.

"Yep, we sure are. But it's those poor devils who will be worst off," replied Jones, pointing to Gallo and his troops. "Tomorrow we start to train them."

Taylor smiled, thinking of the drunken Italians having to slog through his training drills the following morning. Drills he would let his own people forgo to rest from their recent duties. He got to his feet and was pleased to find he wasn't as far gone as some of the others. He walked over to Gallo who reached over to hug him. The short Italian struggled to do so, which only made him laugh.

"You said we'll be training you?" Taylor asked.

"Yes, and an honour it will be!"

"I hope you're ready then, 0800 hours we begin."

Gallo stood back with a puzzled expression. He looked as if someone had just cancelled the party.

"Surely not? This is a time for celebration. We have plenty of time to learn!"

"And if the enemy launch an offensive tomorrow? They start making raids against our landing zones, and we need to fight them off, what would you do?"

"But they won't. We have them boxed in."

"You think so? You think the enemy is completely predictable? Then you know nothing. 0800 hours, Major, have your troops formed up on the parade ground."

He turned and walked away, leaving Gallo speechless. Captain Grey had been watching and was clearly as sober as a judge.

"That was harsh," he said as Taylor walked by, causing him to stop.

He studied the Captain for a moment and was curious that he was not partaking in the festivities.

"Yes it was, but they need to be ready ASAP. No wine, Captain?"

"No, I saw a whole platoon in my regiment killed because they got into a liquor shop and went too far. Somebody needs to stay alert round here."

"There are sentries posted."

"Yes, but not ours. Theirs," he said, pointing to the Italians who were leaping around and making jokes with each other.

"Then you understand my position?"

Grey nodded. They both had to concede that the other was right.

"You haven't told any of us about this training tomorrow. I assume that means you were intending to do it yourself?"

"Yes, let our people have some time out."

"I'll join you. You need a task master, and that's just what I have done for my whole life."

"But you are an officer now."

"No excuse to drill them any lighter. I wasn't born an

officer. Hell, I never asked to be one."

"But you've done a damn fine job of it."

"It's just the job of a sergeant with snazzier uniforms and better pay."

Taylor laughed and nodded in agreement. He'd always had respect for the senior NCOs of his unit, and most others he had met.

"You can join me, if you like. The help would certainly be appreciated."

"I will join you also."

Taylor recoiled slightly in shock to see Jafar standing behind them."

"Jesus."

"You see what I mean," added Grey. "I bet Jafar he couldn't get to within knife distance without you spotting him."

Taylor nodded humbly. It was a harsh lesson the Captain had played on him, and had it been almost anyone else, he'd have been less kind about it. Jafar still awaited his answer.

"Yeah, you'll be damn useful tomorrow. Can you get access to a Mech suit to use for training?"

"Yes," he replied confidently.

"Then it's a date. Time to shake these Italian boys up and get them into fighting shape."

* * *

Taylor looked at his watch. 0800 hours on the dot, and he could see Gallo staggering towards them. His face was pale, and he looked like he got gotten no more than two or three hours sleep. A hundred of his battalion followed him to the drill square. Grey was shaking his head at the display before them.

"Form up!" he yelled.

It was a booming voice that even Taylor couldn't manage.

They shuffled into a vague order, which Grey wasn't impressed with at all.

"Stand up straight!" he shouted.

Taylor lifted his hand to stop the former Sergeant Major before he reverted to old ways and tore them apart for their slack behaviour. Mitch continued.

"I am not here to be your drill sergeant, and I am not here to be your friend. I am here to make you the best you can be in a fight. To give you the best chance of survival in face of the enemy!"

He turned away and walked a few paces back to a doorway of one of the vehicle storage bays that surrounded the grounds. He hit the entry switch, and the door slid open, revealing a rack of Reitech equipment.

"I have ten suits here. These are spare units carried for our Battalion, so look after them. You may use them until your own arrive. I want ten volunteers!"

Despite their drunken and hung-over state, a flurry of

volunteers stepped forward, eager to get their hands on the equipment they had all desired since first setting eyes on it. Mitch grabbed the remote for the dolly rack the equipment lay on and drove it out on the parade ground, pointing for the first ten who had come forward to continue.

They set on the gear like locusts and were quickly strapping themselves in. Many of those still standing watched, yawning and swaying from the lack of sleep and excessive drinking. The volunteers were ready within a few minutes, but as yet had no weapons. Taylor reached down to the dolly and pulled out what looked like the Assegai they carried.

"This is a training version of the Assegai. Same weight and size, but it uses an electric shock through your opponent. It will hurt a human, and even drop them to the ground if it hits bare flesh. To a Mech it will shock them for a second or two."

He passed out the training weapons and then walked over to another door. He hit the button, and it slid open almost causing a heart attack to half of the Italians. A full armoured Mech stood in the entrance. It was the closest they had ever been to one, and they were speechless.

"Don't worry, our own Jafar is at the controls. This is all part of the training exercise. Well, maybe you should worry."

Jafar stepped out into the daylight and stood with Taylor, who even though wore a Reitech suit, was half the size.

"The standard Mech suit is as heavily armoured as light reconnaissance vehicles and some APCs. Only well aimed close range fire can harm them with your current weapons. We soon learned in the first war that what you are using now simply isn't up to the job. I will not teach you how to fight the enemy with your old gear. It would be a waste of time."

"Colonel?" asked Gallo.

"What is it, Major?"

"This is a war of guns, bombs, and artillery, yet you teach us first to fight with, well, a sword."

Several of the Italians sniggered at the response, but Taylor didn't see the funny side of it.

"If you do go to war against this enemy, there will come to a time when you have to face them without a firearm. You mightbe out of ammunition, or not able to change your magazine in time. You may need to take them down quietly. Do not be under any illusions. This weapon was created out of necessity and experience. Think of it as equivalent to the bayonet."

"A what?" joked one of the Italian volunteers.

Taylor strolled up to the man. He looked down for his name, but it had been covered by the Reitech armour. He didn't care.

"You're pretty confident for a man who's never had to face an enemy in battle. I wonder if the hundreds of thousands of young men and women killed in the wars with these aliens shared your same confidence when they met their end?"

The man did not reply.

"This is an enemy who should never be underestimated. The 2nd Inter-Allied have become expert at taking them on, and are now able to punch far greater than their weight would suggest, but that didn't come easy! We lost many friends to get to this point. We are here to help you the easy way so that you may not have to lose lives unnecessarily as a learning curve."

The man swallowed his pride and finally responded.

"Sorry, Sir."

"You will be if you aren't ready when your time comes. For now, you have volunteered yourself to go first. What's your name?"

"Rizzo, Sir," he said cautiously, as he looked at Jafar standing in the hulking Mech suit.

He handed one of the Assegai trainers to the man.

"The Mechs carry large weapons and may try to swing them at you at close quarters, but they are unwieldy. They are more likely to drop their weapons and use the power of their suit. Jafar will begin with open hands, whereas you have a weapon."

Rizzo seemed utterly shocked at the prospect of fighting the metal beast with such a small weapon and having to use his own hands.

"A real Assegai will push right through their armour like a cutting torch, but you have to place a good sturdy thrust into the armour. In this particular situation you, Rizzo, have the advantage. The Mech suit still has a lot of power, but with the Reitech equipment you have speed, flexibility, and a weapon which can bypass their armour entirely when used correctly."

Taylor moved back and gestured for the others to do so, spanning out in a crescent shape to watch. Rizzo's confidence seemed to vanish, as he stood alone against Jafar.

"I have instructed Jafar to simulate the fighting style of one of the common enemy soldiers. He will try to strike and fight as they could, and to minimise the risk of injury. However, be under no illusions, you are in danger."

"But you have not given us any training yet."

Taylor smiled back.

"A few minutes ago you were all too eager to get face to face with the enemy and prove your worth. Clearly, you think yourself up to the task. In order to win here, you must land a thrust into the torso or head armour."

Taylor lifted a shield from the rack and placed it on Rizzo's arm.

"Begin!"

The man formed a basic fighting stance as best he could. Jafar approached quickly and aggressively. Taylor could already see the Italians were shocked to see the strength and power of one of the aliens in action. Rizzo cowered behind the large shield, but Jafar struck him like a bull. Rizzo was launched off his feet and tossed through the air, landing on his back on the hard ground. The suit was all that saved him from spinal injury. The wind was knocked out of him, and he groaned in pain.

"Get up! Jafar may give you the opportunity for a second chance. The enemy will not!" yelled Taylor.

Grey watched on silently. He could see it was a lesson being taught brutally but effectively. Rizzo got to his feet and held the weapon before him. The Assegai was out in front, the blade protruding past the shield as he approached. Jafar swung quickly and smashed the blade with the claw of his armoured suit. The blade flew from Rizzo's grip.

Jafar followed it with a hammer blow from above. Rizzo lifted his shield to stop it, but the power smashed it down and dropped him onto his knees. Before he could recover, Jafar kicked under his shield into his chest, knocking him onto his back again and sent the shield hurtling across the ground with sparks flying up all around.

Rizzo tried to sit up, but Jafar stood on his chest armour and pinned him to the ground. He was helpless.

"Enough!" Taylor ordered.

Jafar released his hold and stood back from the stricken soldier. Taylor stepped forward and hauled him to his feet.

"The first thing you should see here is that you cannot

treat this like you are fighting someone of roughly equal size and strength. This equipment has done wonders, but do not think for a minute that makes you equal. You must use speed and dexterity to overcome their mass and power."

He could see Rizzo was scornful for being shown up so badly. Taylor picked up the shield and Assegai the Private had dropped.

"Use the shield to approach safely against their weapons, and then to divert the energy of their strikes, not take it full on, not unless it is the only thing that will save your life."

He gestured for Jafar to come at him. His alien friend quickly responded and rushed at the Colonel with all the bullish speed and power he had used previously. Taylor stepped just a little off to the side and brushed off a heavy strike from Jafar with his shield, allowing him to tumble on past. As he did, Taylor thrust the Assegai under the shield into the gut.

The electric shock hit and momentarily incapacitated Jafar, sending him crashing face first onto the hard ground. The Italians looked on with shock. They had expected Jafar to give Taylor an easier go of it, but it was a brutal and short fight. Taylor knew Jafar had given it to him easy because he was a far better fighter than any normal alien soldier. He had none of the clumsiness he'd put on.

"You see, you are lighter, faster, and better if you use

their strength against them and your own ability and weapons to your advantage. Rizzo was a perfect example of how much work is needed to get you into fighting shape. And so begins your real training."

* * *

Six months later.

The camp at Naples had expanded tenfold since they arrived, and it was just one of many such troop concentrations which had developed since the new war began. Taylor was walking back to the mess halls from morning exercises when a fresh armoured regiment rolled in. He stood and watched for a few minutes as dozens of armoured vehicles rolled on past. Many were brand new. Others were heavily modified and older. Eventually, he recognised one of the tank commanders on top of one of the vehicles passing him.

"Becker!"

Captain Lukas Becker, and in much better shape than when we last met.

The German Captain looked down and instantly knew Taylor. He spoke into his radio ordering his driver to pull over and out of the column.

"Colonel now?" he asked.

He jumped down from his tank and embraced Taylor with a hug. He could still never get used to such European mannerisms but accepted it as the sign of friendship it was.

"And you, still a Captain. I thought you'd be in charge of the regiment by now."

"I could have perhaps come close to it, but that is not the life for me. Let me worry about my own crew, and that'll do just fine."

"You must be one of the old men of the regiment now."

"Yes, a veteran of more battles than I care to remember, but not as many as you."

"Any news on when all this kicks off?"

"No, but it can't be long now. Every unit I have contact with has been moving to the southern coastline. You may be able to go by air, but much of our armour will have to go by sea."

"So will a lot of our infantry, I'm guessing. With this large a force, we simply won't have enough aircraft for everyone. I'm glad to see you made it through all this and are still fighting on. Last time I saw you, I thought you looked ready to pack it all in."

"Yes, I was, but the enemy had other ideas."

"Well, I'm glad to have you with us."

"Likewise," he said, climbing back onto his tank.

"I'll see you around, Colonel."

He gave a casual salute as the tank rolled on to join the seemingly endless column. Jones appeared at Taylor's side and had just caught sight of Becker as he left.

"Sending German armour to North Africa? Didn't work so well last time."

Taylor had to laugh.

"I wouldn't remind him of that."

"We must be close now."

"Yep, I guess another day or two, and we'll be ready to move."

Just as he said it, a voice came over the loudspeakers mounted around the base.

"All senior officers report to the briefing room, immediately."

"I guess this could be it."

Taylor's hunger from a busy morning completely subsided at the realisation they might finally have news. They rushed to the large briefing room that had been established at the centre of the base. Over fifty officers had assembled, and Commander Phillips stood on the stage with several other higher-ranking officials. Chief among them was General Schulz. Taylor hadn't seen him since the first war had ended, but they seemed to have settled their differences back then. Schulz stood up to address them.

"At 2100 hours tomorrow Operation Freedom will begin. That is the operation to take the fight to the enemy!"

Cheers rang out. Few wanted to have to fight, but all wanted to see and know that an end was in sight. He lifted up his hand to call for silence.

"At 2100 hours the infantry forces stationed here, as well as along many other bases throughout the Mediterranean, will set off for designated landing sites in North Africa. Their deployment will be timed to land just hours before a massive beach landing of armour and additional forces. Be under no illusions, this will be the greatest military operation in the history of the World."

The room fell silent as they took in his words.

"Operational details will be handled at Company and Battalion level and is being organised and dispersed presently. Tomorrow it all begins, and it does not stop until we have seized absolute victory. These bastards have occupied our lands long enough. Let's take them back. I want all of you to rest easy tonight and be ready for the road that lies ahead. That'll be all."

They all exited the room in a stunned state. All thought of the day to come and knew they wouldn't sleep that night.

"You really think this is it?" asked Jones.

"Yes. We've given those boys all the training we can. We have amassed all the forces we can. It's time to move."

"You think it'll be enough."

"Sure, why not? We fought the first war on their terms in their time. This time we do it on ours."

The night passed slowly with little sleep for any of them. Everyone knew the time was nigh. Some hoped for a delay, but most wanted it to begin now. The fact they had to go to the enemy was certain. It was time to get it over and done with. When the sun rose, the camp was eerily quiet. There was no time left for training. They were the best prepared they could be.

At 2000 hours the megaphone sounded. The Battalion had been sitting in the warmth of the evening outside their billets, coffee and tea their only comfort.

"All personnel to begin boarding and prepare for take off."

Taylor looked down at his watch.

"The ships must already be at the coast by now."

"Then let's hope that armour gets ashore."

They had poured over intelligence gathered from the enemy positions for weeks and months, and now it was time to finally act.

I only hope we're right about it all.

"Let's move!"

The order was carried on down the line, as the base was becoming a sudden hive of activity. He strode for Eddie's copter, knowing the pilot was always waiting to be his personal pilot. It brought him a sense of security to have Eddie at the controls. They had been shot down and gone through hell together more than a few times, but they always survived.

As he climbed aboard, he looked down at his Mappad to study the area one last time. The allied landings would be taking place along the coast of Tunisia from Gabes to Tripoli, but their job was to go beyond in the largest airborne operation in history.

CHAPTER ELEVEN

Gabes, another city I've never heard of, despite spending weeks preparing an operation there, Taylor thought.

He'd poured over photos and maps to the extent he felt he was intimately familiar with the land.

"Two minutes!" said Rains.

Anti-aircraft pulses burst in the sky before them and were increasing at a rapid rate. The massive aerial offensive was hopefully enough to hold back their air power. For the Battalion and all the others in the sky, they could only wait and hope. He couldn't see anything from his seat, but neither did he want to. Their time finally came.

"Thirty seconds!"

"Line up!" ordered Taylor.

They were all glad to be getting out of the copter. They'd rather face the enemy themselves than wait to be blown out of the sky. Their job was to secure the land north of Gabes, a narrow patch corridor between the salt lake Chott el Jerid and the sea. It was the opposite end of the offensive to where the ruins of the K'til lay, but he knew it was vitally important until they had secured a beachhead.

There'll be plenty of time yet to find Demiran.

He counted down on his watch as they all stood and approached the door.

"Good luck to you all," he said through comms.

Several nodded in agreement. Jones was first at the door. Taylor was halfway down the line with Jafar at his back. The green light at the door lit up, and Jones leapt without hesitation. The rest of the platoon followed him. As Taylor reached the door, he realised how dark the area was. There was no lighting on the ground. The moon provided minimal amounts. Only the enemy pulses and explosions provided streaks and bursts around them.

He stopped at the door for only a second and jumped. The copters had been flying at just over two hundred metres from the dusty surface, so it was a quick descent. His boosters lit up the space beneath him as they dropped. It quickly become apparent they were landing right on top of a complex system of enemy trenches which had not shown up in any of their intelligence reports and satellite imagery. He could only assume they covered it by day, but there was no time to worry about that now.

Pulses raced up at them from the enemy positions

below, and far more fire was sent down from the airborne as they descended. Inter-Allied, and Italian forces from 3rd and 4th Mechanized Infantry formed their 5th Brigade. It was the first time the Italians had seen combat, but Taylor was confident they would hold their own.

He was approaching a Mech at high speed, despite his boosters slowing him rapidly. The creature was firing up at several of his comrades. He opened fire with his rifle and got off three shots before landing on top of the alien. His weight smashed it off its feet. He quickly got up and could see his shots had killed it before he'd even landed.

A quick assessment of his surroundings found he stood inside thick concrete-like trenches. They were three metres wide by two deep, tall enough so that he could not see out over the top. He jumped up onto the body of the Mech to get some view all around. As he did so, he caught a glimpse of an enemy Mech advancing around a bend in the trench, but before he could respond, gunfire ripped into the soldier. He looked up. Jafar was above the trench and firing in.

Gunfire sounded all around; more of theirs than the enemy. Jafar jumped down in the trench to his side.

"Why the hell didn't we know about these positions?" Taylor asked.

Jafar seemed as baffled as him. Several of Jones' platoon joined him.

"All right, let's sweep and clear."

He lifted up his rifle and continued on down the line. The first thing they encountered were three Mechs firing over the trench line at the incoming friendlies. They fired several bursts, moving in on the aliens, killing them before they could respond.

"At least it looks like we did actually catch them by surprise. Thanks to you, no doubt," he said to Jafar. He'd been instrumental in their counter-intelligence operations leading up to the invasion.

They continued north along the line of defences and found little resistance until they reached the farthest point of the trenches looking out north. Taylor reached for a flare from his webbing and fired it up into the sky. They saw open barren land for as far as the light extended.

The gunfire in their location was already calming down, but they could hear the battle raging a few kilometres away at the coastline. Jones finally found the Colonel and had a look of utter shock about him.

"Surely it can't be this easy?"

"No, it can't, and it won't be. We could have attacked anywhere, so they would have had to spread thin to defend the borders and coastline. Now they know we're here, they'll come for us with everything they've got."

"How long do you think we have?" asked Jones.

"Not long at all. This is where they'll hit us. Get our anti-tank guns deployed along this line, and find out how the beach operations are going."

Jafar stood silently, looking out into the pitch-black wasteland to the north.

"Maybe we did hit them with overwhelming numbers. They must be weakened from the fight in the east. "

"Yes, they are, but not finished, Charlie."

"No, never underestimate a wounded animal."

They waited in the trenches for an hour before Jones received solid information.

"Most of the beaches have been taken, supply lines are being established, and the armour should be with us within a few hours."

"Then let's hope that's soon enough."

As he said it, they heard the sound they feared the most, heavy tracks from an armoured column advancing from the north.

"They better be quick!" yelled Taylor, lifting his binoculars and switching to night vision. Across the open flat plain, he could just make out the vehicles which were over ten kilometres out and merely silhouettes at present."

"How long do we have?" asked Taylor.

"Maybe twenty minutes."

"Get those guns ready!"

There was nothing more to do but wait for the enemy and await reinforcement. They carried magnetic mines for taking on the tanks if the trenches were over run, but all prayed they would not have to use them. The time seemed to pass quickly. Taylor sat beside one of the portable anti-tank weapons they had brought with them. It was as large as a man and needed two to carry it. They had just a dozen of the weapons within the Brigade.

"Concentrate fire on the two targets given. I want them to think we're punching above our weight," he said into his comm.

"Six guns on two vehicles?" asked Jones.

"I'd rather be sure to nail two than risk spreading our fire. They need to think we've got a lot more here than we have."

"You don't think we can hold against them?"

"Not without armour, no. I can see dozens of tanks heading our way, and I bet there are many more en route."

"How about the airborne armour?"

"It's nowhere to be seen, is it?"

"Bugger."

They had entered into range. Taylor looked down the trench, and the troops were almost shoulder-to-shoulder.

"Fire!" he yelled.

The six guns fired almost in perfect synchronisation. He looked through his binoculars to see one smashed by the fire with two holes having direct hits on the centre of its hull. The other vehicle seemed to brush off the fire and kept moving.

"Shit," he whispered to himself. "Reload!"

The crews were already well ahead of him.

"All fire to be directed on previous target."

The first enemy tanks opened fire and pulses smashed into the ground before and after Taylor's trench.

"Fire!"

The salvo struck the enemy tank, five out of the six shots landed, crippling the vehicle immediately. Smoke belched from its cracked hull.

"Reload and fire in your own time."

Two more of the enemy vehicles fell soon after, but they were now within a kilometre of the trenches and showed no signs of stopping. The intensity of the bombardment was increasing, and dozens of casualties were being reported in the nearby positions alone.

"God save us if they reach here," said Jones.

Taylor pulled out one of the magnetic charges, but it seemed a near hopeless situation if it came to the point of using it. He hunkered down to the trench edge and held the mine ready to deploy. The ground began to shake as they approached.

"Five hundred metres!" warned Jones.

Then their hearts almost stopped as lights flashed to the east, and the cannon fire rang out. Taylor could see a tank regiment approaching and firing with everything they had. He turned back to the battlefield. Half a dozen enemy vehicles were smashed beyond recognition in the initial salvo. Cheers rang out across the trench lines as the enemy advance ground to a halt.

The battle raged on for two hours amongst the armour.

They could do little but appreciate the cover they had inherited and hunker down to wait for it all to be over. By midnight, all had gone quiet, and both sides began to settle in till morning. It was just half an hour into the peacefulness when Jones got out his stove and began to brew up. Taylor smiled as he propped himself up against a trench wall nearby. The excitement of the initial attack was over. For once they had gotten it easy.

"Jafar thinks they'll be falling back through the night," he said.

"I would if I were them. They must have spread themselves thin over thousands of kilometres of shoreline. We're closing in on them now. They must know the end is in sight."

"And yet they still came. They came to Earth with too little, too late," replied Taylor.

"They didn't come for a stand up fight at all, remember. They're trying to survive us, not the other way around."

It was true, and for the first time Taylor was starting to realise how scared they must be, just as they had been in the first war.

"I want Demiran before this is over."

"You and the rest of the world, Mitch."

"No, he's rightfully ours. I want to see that son of a bitch bleed, and I want to see him die at the hands of one of ours."

"We usually get pushed to the front, so there's a good

chance of it."

"Chance? That's not good enough."

"There is a way of finding him."

The two of them were shocked to hear Jafar's voice. It came from up over the trench into the darkness that divided them from the enemy. He jumped down from the edge into the trench. They were both glad his abilities were put to good use with them, as he was a league apart from the regular Mech infantry.

"Go on," said Taylor.

"I know the way he thinks, and I know the way he plans. If I could get a view of their positions, in maybe just an hour or two, I'd know."

"But they must surely be moving constantly."

"If you could get me overhead of the K'til and the positions they have setup there, I could identify Demiran's location by morning."

"But how long would he be wherever you find him?" asked Jones.

"A day, maybe two."

"It could be enough."

"We can't move anywhere without orders."

"Armoured divisions will be heading north at first light. Our job here is done. We'll be heading southeast to take on the main force," replied Taylor.

"Well, probably, but not like we know for sure."

"Sure enough," he said, turning to Jafar.

"So with a little time of aerial surveillance, you reckon you can find him?"

Jafar nodded.

"I can't get you much. Rains is probably crazy enough for it, and one of the only pilots who would do so without asking questions."

"Mitch, you're treading on dangerous ground here, very dangerous."

"What are we doing here? We came here to end Demiran and rid our world of the enemy. What if we could do that in a day, or a week?"

"Then we take it to Phillips, who will take it to those who have the authority to make that happen. I was reckless once, and you know that almost cost me my life. Don't do this alone."

"I'm not doing it alone. I'm asking you to come with me, all of you. We find where Demiran is, and take this brigade right for him."

"The numbers don't add up. We can't take on the might of their entire armies."

"We won't. We're going for Demiran. Just him."

Jones shook his head realising Taylor would not be swayed.

"Get Rains down here. I want that information before first light."

Jones had to accept it because no matter what, he would support his friend. In little over an hour, Jafar was lifting off aboard the copter. The rest lay in their trenches and waited. There was no sign of the enemy that night, only the sound of the odd trade of fire between the armour ahead of them.

"Tomorrow we'll be ordered south to take on Demiran's main forces around the K'til."

"And you intend to speed up that process, Mitch?" Charlie asked.

Parker had been sitting with them for a while, and she joined the conversation.

"And an opportunity to end Demiran's life. When we killed Karadag, they were beaten," Taylor said.

"I didn't say he didn't need to die. If I thought it were that easy, I'd be all for it. But we are one Battalion. Even if we could get the rest of the Brigade aboard, it'll be crazy odds."

"The rest of the Brigade will follow, Charlie. They will follow because it's us. Our reputation means to a lot to them, and I bet it means a lot to Demiran too."

"What do you mean?" asked Parker. "Oh, no, no, no, no. You want to draw him out. You want to bait him with the great champions who killed his kin. You're more crazy than I thought."

"And why not? He wants a piece of me. I want a piece of him. Can't we settle this properly?"

"If he could, he'd order you killed in a heartbeat."

"No he won't. He won't because he has too much pride

for that. He came to destroy this world through bitter hatred. The only thing he hates just as much is me. He knows who I am."

"Wait, this isn't what I signed up for," replied Parker.

"No, you signed up to the Marine Corps, to do your duty," snapped Taylor.

"And what if you're wrong?" she asked.

"Then we fight on no matter. Our armies are heading for the K'til. All this can do is accelerate that path. Who knows what they could be planning? A lightning attack to bring this to a close is exactly what we need."

"And what do you believe will happen to the hundreds of thousands of Mechs if and when you do kill Demiran?" asked Jones.

"I bet their number isn't what it was when they got here. Without him, they'd scatter. Those who could will probably leave Earth on any ships still operational. Though they probably won't make it past our grid and Navy. The rest will scatter across the continent and be mopped up in time."

"Are you that confident that the death of their leader is enough to finish them?"

"I saw it in Jafar and Tsengal, Eli. Demiran died to them the minute he showed his true self and they had a way out."

"I sure hope you're right."

She knew there was no good arguing with him any

longer.

Nothing more was said on the subject until Jafar returned, but the first they knew of it was the sight of him and Rains traipsing across the tops of the trenches towards them.

"They're back," said Parker.

"They survived," added Jones.

"But have they got what we need?"

"I tell you what, this is the last time I fly under this crazy bastard's command!" yelled Eddie.

"Did you get the information? Do you know where Demiran is?"

Mitch could already tell they did.

"Yes, and it was easier than expected," replied Jafar.

"What d'you mean?"

"Son of a bitch is in his quarters aboard the K'til, right where he was when this all began," added Eddie.

"This for real?"

Jafar nodded.

"But why?"

"Unfinished business," added Jones.

Taylor turned in surprise to see Charlie was really onto something.

"He's been waiting for you. This is personal."

"So why don't we just bomb the crap out of him now?" asked Parker.

"No, I want to know this scumbag is dead. I want visual

confirmation, confirmation with my own eyes. Even if we could succeed with a bombing of the target, we'd have to obliterate the area beyond all recognition. I want to see Demiran dead, and then I want the whole World so see him that way, both races."

"Isn't this getting a little too personal?" asked Parker.

"You're damn right it is," added Rains.

Taylor was surprised to see the pilot so vocal and determined.

"I lost one of my best friends because of this bastard, one in a long line of losses since they invaded Earth. I'm with you."

It was just a few hours to sunrise, but before they could make a decision, new orders came in to Taylor's Mappad. He lifted it up to carefully study the map and information given.

"We're heading southeast, just as we thought. The K'til is a few hundred kilometres south of Tripoli."

Nobody spoke for a moment as they considered the possibilities of what Taylor's plan could involve. He looked around to each of their faces. One by one they slowly nodded in agreement.

"Allright, then let's do this. Let's kill this bastard and be done with it!"

He lifted his comm.

"5th Brigade form at my position and prepare for immediate pickup."

It was close to lunchtime when their copters were reaching the frontline. Rains looked to Taylor, uncertain of their orders.

"Put us down here as ordered."

"I thought we were going for Demiran?"

"We are, but not like this. We'll never make it to the K'til. She may be a wreck, but she's still death trap. I want Demiran to come to us."

"Whatever you say, Boss."

Jones seemed to recover his faith in Taylor with these words.

"I thought you were leading them right for us," he whispered.

"I said I wanted to go kill him, not on his terms though."

Jones could see Taylor was being deliberately vague. What concerned him was he wasn't sure if Taylor had a great idea or was making it up as he went along. They heard the roar of engines and dozens of copters flew into view.

"Your boys?" Jones asked Eddie Rains.

"Hell, yeah, I knew the Colonel wouldn't be staying put."

It's all moving so fast, but I can't see any way of slowing things down. The wars have gone on long enough. Maybe Taylor can end them in a day. Just maybe, but is he crazy enough to do what is needed? I suspect so.

"If we do this, we do it together, and we do not stop

until Demiran lies dead before us," Taylor said.

"Exactly what I had in mind," Rains laughed.

"5th Brigade, load up, we're outta here," Taylor ordered.

When Jones and Taylor finally sat down in the copter, with at least a little privacy behind the cockpit, Taylor brought up his Mappad.

"Friendly units have moved a hundred kilometres south through the night."

"A hundred kilometres? They'd have to be going all out."

"From what I can see the enemy forces were amassed in three places. The K'til, with their leader, the far north of Tunisia and Algeria where they would have expected our assault, and at the walls of Jerusalem."

"So we've pushed through an opening, but what happens when they begin to close in around us?"

"With the taking of southern Tunisia, it was guaranteed there would be a drive north to stop the enemy from regrouping with those at the K'til. This is the reason we were no longer needed in Gabes. And I have no doubt the armies in Jerusalem will show no mercy in pursuing the enemy at their walls, should they try and run. The enemy is spread thin and weak."

"But we both know Demiran could still be dangerous."

Just after sunrise they put down in the Libyan Desert. It was a flat and barren landscape with little cover of any note. But as Taylor stepped out from the copter, he was met with an imposing and horrifying sight, the crash site of the larger part of the K'til. Even at fifty kilometres south, it still dominated the landscape. Allied artillery had already begun a bombardment, but they were positioned a kilometre away, so it was a dull muted drone.

To their front they could see three lines of trenches that had clearly been dug just a few hours before during the night.

"These boys can't have had a lot of rest."

"Not like they use shovels anymore," replied Taylor.

"No, but to have made it this far in this quickly. They must have met at least some resistance."

Out of the corner of his eye, Taylor noticed an officer and his contingent approaching. He turned to see that it was Colonel Harney with Commander Phillips. There would be no saluting, now that they were at the frontline.

"'Morning!" yelled Taylor.

"Welcome to the front," replied Harney.

He could see Harney was more than a little pleased with himself. He strutted about as if he had claimed a massive victory. But Taylor knew they were where they were now not through hard fighting the past few months, but good planning.

"Good work on getting so far," he replied sedately and turned to Phillips.

"Sir, this was a fine display of intelligence and organisation."

"Thank you, Colonel."

"What do we do now?"

"We might have made it this far, but now we come up against the largest of Demiran's three armies, most likely with him at the head of it. It has become clear that many of the anti-aircraft systems aboard the K'til are once more operational, and that makes it dangerous to approach from the air. The first Navy boys who did were blasted out of the sky. So, this'll be a ground fight. We advance as much as we can when we able to until they have nowhere else to go."

"You think they'll stand and fight now we're here?" asked Harney.

Taylor did not have to respond. Jafar did so for him.

"While Demiran lives, they will fight to the very end for him."

"No one ever thought of stabbing him in the back?" Jones asked.

Harney looked to the Captain with disgust, for he knew the thought alone could be enough to cause chaos among their own armies.

"If soldiers repeatedly killed their leaders, where would we be?"

"Beg your pardon, Sir. But Demiran isn't you or I. He is a ruthless dictator who would have seen the utter destruction of our race. I can't find any remorse or sympathy for his situation."

Harney had read Jones' file and gave him some leeway as a result.

"So, enemy positions and strength?" asked Taylor.

"They're just over a kilometre ahead of us in the same trenches we saw at the coast, but in much greater number," replied Phillips.

"Below ground, they'll be a tough nut to crack," added Jones.

"Yep. That armour they wear is thick, and with the cover of trenches, our artillery will have a hard time shifting them. I doubt the psychological effects will mean much to them."

"They fear death and injury, but are too scared to disobey their orders," replied Jafar.

"Colonel, you're to dig in here and await further orders. We'll take ground at every opportunity and make new defensives quickly and at regular intervals. We know how detrimental trench warfare can be to both sides. This war may be in its final stages, but it will not be over soon."

Don't be so sure, thought Taylor.

"Carry on, Colonel."

They carried on down the line. Taylor looked on to see the trench positions they had been given were manned by just a single detachment from Harney's Fighting Fifth. They were at the front trench, and he could already see they wouldn't be keen to give it up. They had been given a stretch of land half a kilometre long, meaning they'd be tight on space.

"Into the trenches," Taylor said across the comms.

Many had been expecting to get into the thick of the fighting and make the enemy suffer. They paced enthusiastically over to the defences, realising how long the war could go on for once both sides were entrenched. Taylor turned back to Rains who stood at the ramp of his copter.

"I believe your war is over, Lieutenant. Fall back to the staging area five clicks north of here. You may be needed yet when the casualties start piling up."

"Can't say I'm sad to be benched, Colonel. Good luck out there."

He stepped aboard and was quickly firing up the engines to lift off. Taylor turned back south; most of the Brigade was at the edges of the trenches and piling in to what many expected to be their homes for some time. He had other ideas. He turned to Jafar at his side.

"Tell me you have a way of contacting Demiran?"

"There is a way, why?"

"He may not want to dirty his hands in this war, but I know exactly how to call him out."

"You think you can force him out here? Then what?"

"Then we kill him, and anyone who stands in our way."

Jafar smiled. He already liked the sound of the plan.

"Make it happen. I want to talk to him myself, and I don't care who sees it."

"This isn't going to be the long drawn out fight Phillips thinks, is it?"

Taylor stepped forward and noticed Jones had been standing the other side of Jafar, and so obscured by the alien.

"No, not at all. This ends here and now."

CHAPTER TWELVE

Demiran lay back in his throne aboard the stricken wreck of the K'til. He still could not believe he had fallen so far. He was slumped and lost. He wanted nothing more than to leave Earth for good and return home, but he knew with so little left, he would be torn apart by the other Lords. He suspected Erdogan would have already claimed his homeworld if news had gotten back to Tau Ceti of his plight. Six months since the destruction of the K'til, and he had made no progress. He had the look of a soldier who was utterly beaten.

A projection suddenly appeared before him. Used only by his close counsel, he sat up quickly when he realised who was addressing him. Taylor stood just five metres from his throne. The projection was near perfect with only minimal transparency. He had not seen the Colonel since his time in captivity, but he knew exactly who he was.

"I am Colonel Taylor of the 2nd Inter-Allied."

Demiran stood up, and his back straightened as he felt hatred invigorate him.

"Your time is coming to an end. Your fleet is destroyed, and your armies are surrounded. Your Planet Killer is finished."

"What do you want?" he asked.

"I want to kill you like the dog you are."

"And what makes you think you could?"

"Because I killed Karadag. With my own hands."

Demiran's eyes widened at the news. It was clear he did not know Taylor had been the one to do it.

"It was you who ended my kinsman's life and mission, and you who imprisoned me. You, who did this to the Gezgen K'til! You, who have turned one of my own against me. I am going to kill you before this is over!"

Taylor could see the alien's blood boiling and smiled to only fuel it further.

"Come and try."

The creature screamed in fury as it grabbed a table beside his throne and launched it across the room in anger.

"I'll be waiting," added Taylor confidently and ending the transmission.

Jones breathed out an uneasy sigh, thinking about what Taylor had just done.

"You've baited a dangerous opponent."

"Do you want this war to go on another six months?

We'll lose thousands, maybe tens of thousands of soldiers if this war goes on. What if it could be ended in just one bloody day?"

"I'm not sure that was your decision to make."

"Well, tough shit."

"This is Taylor to the 5th Brigade. Prepare for combat. We have incoming."

He could see that many around him appeared surprised. There was no sign of movement as yet, but they readied their weapons as ordered. A few minutes passed, as Taylor stood on the flat plain above the trenches, watching south. Eventually, his Mappad began to flash, and he lifted it to see enemy advances all across the front. Phillips had been walking the line when he rushed to Taylor's position.

"Looks like they're coming at us."

"Damn right, Sir. They're out for blood. This isn't going to be a meat grinder. This ends in one pitched battle."

"What? How do you know?"

Taylor smiled.

"You did this? You riled up Demiran like you do every leader, haven't you?"

"It wasn't difficult."

"God damn you, Taylor, this better work."

"Don't worry, it will."

"Christ," he uttered, rushing off to get to HQ.

Taylor knew he would be in deep trouble for what he had done, but nobody had time to do anything about it.

The Mappad showed enemy advances over ten kilometres of the front.

"He's coming," stated Taylor.

"Yes, are you ready?" asked Jafar.

"Have to be. Demiran had you as a bodyguard, am I to assume there are others like you that will do the same?"

"Yes, always four, and always from my homeworld. They will not be so easily swayed to our cause as Tsengal and I were."

"No, those were exceptional circumstances. But it does mean we'll have to take them on also."

"Yes."

Taylor was expecting some kind of emotion, but he appeared to show none. He turned and glared at his friend until he provoked a response.

"I would hope they would join us, and I would never wish to kill my own. They were brothers to me once, just as you are now. But I will not hesitate to do what needs to be done."

It was all the confirmation Taylor needed. Though he still was uneasy about the thought of four bodyguards of Jafar's calibre surrounding Demiran. His Mappad flashed as fresh orders came through.

"Hold position."

They would do so for now, but no one was in charge of Taylor any longer. He knew what he must do for himself and all who had fought from the beginning. He stepped up to the front trench and Jones followed suit.

"You can't fight him alone," stated Jones.

"I don't intend to."

"You just issued a personal challenge."

"I did no such thing. All I did was piss him off enough to want to come and deal with me himself. If he assumes this is gonna be one-on-one, then he's a fool. Anyway, when have they ever played so honourably? No, he'll come with everything he can get. He must know his war is over. It's just a matter of time. Killing me is the only thing left he could achieve."

"Let's see it doesn't happen then. As reckless as you can be, I've grown rather fond of you, Mitch."

"Don't go all soft on my now, Charlie? Where's the fire in you?"

"It's coming, don't you worry."

They watched the enemy amassing in the distance. As far as the eye could see in either direction, they were coming.

"Could this really be it? The last battle to end it all?" asked Jones.

"It's about time. We've been fighting this long enough."

Taylor reached down to his comms unit and set it to a private channel to just their own battalion.

"This is Taylor. Somewhere amongst that army is Demiran. Lord Demiran who came to destroy the human race, the same bastard who escaped us and has been the cause of millions of deaths. He is coming for us because he knows who the 2nd Inter-Allied are. He knows our reputation, and he knows what we have done. What he doesn't know is what we are still capable of."

He went quiet for a moment and turned to see many were thinking hard about what he was saying.

"You have all sacrificed a lot in this war, and the war before it. But I ask you now to follow me. Let's end this today. We could fight on and sees tens of thousands die before the year is done, or you can follow me to victory today. I don't say it'll be easy. But if you do so with the same courage I have seen from the beginning, I can guarantee you, I will kill that son of a bitch and end this war!"

He hadn't said what or how he intended to do it, but it was clear to many. He looked around to see plenty were nodding in approval. Then he caught Eli Parker's gaze, and a single tear dropped down her face. They both knew it could cost them dearly to succeed in what he was intending, but she would not be the one to stop him.

"So I need to know. I can't do this alone, are you with me?"

Jones nodded in agreement, but he knew the Captain would follow him no matter what.

"Damn right," came the reply from Jackson.

"Yes, Sir, all the way," added Ota.

"As always, we trust you to see this through, we are with you," said Grey.

Thank God. He knew he had to take the fight to Demiran with their support or not.

"There's always time to reconsider," said Jones.

"No, my mind is made up, Charlie. I won't have this battle descend into a month of bitter bloodshed."

He lifted his intercom.

"Then keep a keen eye for Demiran. He is the key to it all. Be ready for him."

It wasn't long before the massive enemy armies were reaching their own trench works and passing them. They were reaching noon, and the heat was becoming intoxicating. The enemy advance began to grow as they reached their frontline, and a dust cloud was forming at their backs like a storm bearing down on the allied defences.

Artillery began to roar behind them, and the armour dug in also joined the fight. They could see the enemy had little in the way of heavy armour. What had survived the crash of the K'til had largely been expended in the folly attempt to take Jerusalem. The sun glinted off the tens of thousands of Mech suits that they could see. They approached as a wall across the desert.

"Five hundred metres," said Jones.

"Prepare to fire in your own time," ordered Taylor.

"Four hundred metres."

"Steady."

"Three fifty!"

"Fire!

The opening volley was deafening as the enemy front was smashed. Every one of the Brigade took well-aimed shots, and the effect was devastating. And yet they still came.

"Two hundred metres!"

Taylor slammed in a new magazine and kept firing. He knew Demiran couldn't be far from the line they were firing on, as he would be actively seeking Mitch out. The second magazine emptied. Just a hundred and fifty metres out, Taylor caught a glimpse of something standing out in their lines; blackened armour, that of Demiran and his personal retinue. They quickly disappeared again as Mech infantry formed around them to keep moving forward.

"This is it," said Taylor. "Our opportunity is finally here."

"What are you doing, Mitch?" asked Jones hesitantly.

"2nd Inter-Allied. Lord Demiran lies ahead of us. This is our chance. This is our time to make him pay for everything he has done."

Taylor leapt out of the trench, turning his back to the enemy.

"I'm going to kill that bastard! Who's with me?" he shouted.

"Oh, hell," Jones muttered.

The Battalion arose almost like clockwork from the trenches, leaping out onto the open plain and rushing forward with their shields held before them to cover the advance.

Phillips couldn't miss the shocking sight from his position behind the lines with Harney. They were in an armoured command truck two kilometres back.

"What the hell is he doing?"

Harney rushed to the screen and shouted at an operator beside it.

"Zoom in there!"

"Demiran, it's him," replied Phillips.

Harney turned, looking at the Commander utterly puzzled.

"He thinks he can finish this. Crazy fool."

"Yes, but our crazy fool, and one who actually has some chance of doing it."

He moved to order the rest of the Brigade forward, but it was too late, they had already followed the Colonel. Gallo was at the head of his battalion, only a few metres short of Taylor.

"Get the Fifth forward, immediate advance!" screamed Phillips.

Harney hesitated for a moment, for it seemed like suicide.

"Do it!"

"This is Colonel Harney, advance. Advance now!"

Taylor's Battalion was covering the ground at a rapid pace, and his shield had already brushed off two pulses when he got halfway. He pushed his rifle out to the side between his and Jafar's shield to fire as they advanced. A wall of fire they were defenceless against hit the Mechs' advance. But the first few shields were breaking under the weight of the enemy fire, and he knew they had to get past it quickly. He saw a dozen of their own fall around them and knew they'd have taken many more casualties covering the open ground.

Mitch activated his boosters and leapt ten metres off the ground, launching himself at the frontline of Mechs. He landed hard against the first one, one foot on the ground, and the other on the Mech's torso where he had smashed it to the ground. Before it could recover, he fired a burst into its head.

Jafar surged past him and barged into the next alien in his way. The nimble and strong alien ducked under one of the Mech's weapons and impeded an Assegai into the faceplate of another. Taylor looked back to their lines for just a second and could see thousands of troops rushing forwards to assist them. Many more were clambering out of the trenches to join in. He didn't know whether the order had been given of not, but it had gotten the effect he wanted.

Few could stand and do nothing when they saw the charge led by Taylor himself. Gallo was scared to death, and yet he still charged for the enemy beside the 2nd Inter-Allied.

"This is it, they're coming!" he yelled.

He turned back to the fight and saw a pulse rushing towards him. Jones jumped into the path of it, and the pulse burst over his shield, sending the debris shattering around both of them.

"This is your chance! Let's do it!" Jones shouted out.

Taylor stepped off the body of his first victim and strode forward. He could see Jafar had got ahead of them and cut down another two before they could reach him. A pulse hit Taylor's rifle as he progressed into the enemy ranks, and it was shattered in two. He unclipped it from his armour, let it drop to the ground, and drew his Assegai. Monty and Blinker were close by their side and jumped forward to help. Blinker ducked down but was hit full force by one of their cannons. It hit his face and snapped his neck.

Monty didn't hesitate and jumped forward, driving his Assegai deep into the Mech. The blade entered at its stomach and drove up into its chest, running the hilt up to its armour. He pulled out the bloodied blade and could see his brother was already dead. He had no words for it, only rushed on forward to join Taylor in the killing.

Jones' platoon smashed their way through three more ranks of Mechs, losing just a few of their own when Taylor finally came to a halt. Demiran stood ten metres away with his four bodyguards. He pulled off his helmet so he could gaze upon Taylor with his own eyes. A massive glaive was held in one of his hands, and he was clearly there for only one purpose. His bodyguards all carried the same weapon. Taylor looked to his side. Silva was with them, and Yorath led a platoon on his other side.

He looked back to the alien leader. The sun reflected off the gold decoration of his blackened armour. He could see a large scar down the alien's face. It had not been there when he had been their prisoner. Demiran lifted his glaive and gave out a loud roar as he rushed forward.

Taylor didn't have to say a word. Twenty of the Inter-Allied soldiers with him rushed forwards. Monty was at the front and clearly after some payback. As he approached the first bodyguard, he went into a roll and smashed the alien's legs with his shield, forcing it to tumble into a dive towards the rest of them. Jafar smashed the creature down into the dirt, bringing it to an abrupt halt and stabbed it three times in the back.

Monty was back on his feet and immediately took a blow to his shield. He thrust up against the bodyguard, but his arm was hit down, and the glaive spiralled around in the creature's grip until it connected with his neck and took his head clean off. Taylor was on the creature next and used his boosters to leap up and strike the bodyguard in the face with the edge of the shield; then his bodyweight to drive it down to the ground. He thrust his Assegai into its eye socket while it lay stunned. The blade drove right through its skull and onto the ground.

The next creature kicked him off, but Silva and Jones smashed it back with their shields. Demiran reached them, and with all his power swung the glaive over his head and down onto Silva. He lifted his shield, but the massive blade cut it in two and removed his hand at the wrist while knocking him down onto his back. Jones tried to strike forward, but he pendulumed the blade over his head and struck with all his force horizontally. Jones' shield buckled, and he was thrown away like a ragdoll.

Demiran rushed forward to move onto Taylor who was getting back to his feet, but Jafar came from his side. He thrust quickly, but Demiran noticed in time and stepped away from him. Jafar followed with a series of quick and brutal thrusts that Demiran knocked aside. The massive glaive moved at rapid speed with the leverage and power he wielded it with. One of the bodyguards jumped in to help his Lord, but Taylor seized the opportunity and smashed his shield into the creature's kneecap. Not even its armour was enough to save it from the fierce strike that sent it crashing down onto the body of one of the others.

Taylor thrust his weapon forward, but it was beaten aside as the alien turned, stopping his attack with its glaive held across its body. He landed on top of the creature to stop it moving the weapon any further. They were locked and unable to move. The bodyguard released one of its hands and swung a punch to his head, but he moved quickly, and it brushed his helmet. He looked back to see an Assegai imbedded in its head. Yorath was wielding the blade.

Before he could thank the young officer, a glaive pierced through his chest and spurt red blood over Taylor. Yorath released his grip on the Assegai imbedded in the creature's head and fell. Taylor drew out the blade and jumped up at the creature with a long thrust. It evaded and knocked him away with the shaft of its weapon. But it landed against two of John's platoon. They thrust their blades into its back, killing it where it stood.

Taylor could see Jafar and Demiran locked in battle. Blood poured from Jafar's face, and a deep cut ran from his shoulder and almost to his hip. Demiran didn't have any visible injuries, but he was being pressed hard. Mitch rushed to help. Jafar ducked under one strike and jumped forward to drive his shield up against the glaive and hold it away. He thrust his Assegai quickly into Demiran's stomach, and the alien screeched out loud in pain. Demiran reached down and pulled the weapon from his belly, throwing it aside in disgust.

He kicked Jafar back, swung the glaive about his head, and brought it down hard. Jafar managed to pass the strike off with his shield, but Demiran brought the bottom ball weight around and onto his head. The strike landed so hard it smashed Jafar off his feet and down into the dirt. He lay lifeless among the dead.

Taylor stopped at the sight of it, doubting for a moment

if he could beat the towering enemy Lord. He saw the Mechs all around had stopped to watch the fight, and the allies were doing likewise. Demiran yelled something in his own language to his soldiers. There was no response. They remained mesmerised by the fight.

Jones staggered to his feet and stumbled over to Taylor. He could barely walk from the multiple broken ribs and arm.

"What are they doing?" asked Taylor.

"Starting to see it. That they are going to lose. You have to do this."

Fear overcame Taylor when he saw what was being expected of him. The enemy wanted to see Demiran defeated in single combat. It was the one thing that could save countless lives on both sides. He looked down to Demiran's wound. Blood still gushed from it, and he limped a few paces as a result.

I pray Jafar did enough damage to give me a fighting chance.

"Taylor, slaver of Karadag. You could not have killed such a great Lord alone. You are weak, small, and insignificant," spat Demiran.

Taylor knew he could not show his fear.

"And yet here we are. Your death imminent, just as your kinsman died. Your people do not want to fight for you. With your death, it will be over, your entire legacy."

That angered Demiran, and he spat out on the ground. But his spit was blood from the wound.

"No, you will die at my hands, just as Colonel Chandra did."

Taylor looked into his eyes and could see he was telling the truth. It only enraged him further.

"Then it was surely she who left you that scar?"

Demiran hissed, and it was clearly true. Taylor smiled.

"You hear that? Chandra gave him that wound! He thinks me small, but he was bled by a woman who stood half his height!"

It pleased him to know so, and he knew it would do the same for the whole Battalion.

She wouldn't have died without a vicious last fight.

A Mech pushed and shoved to get through the ranks and slid back its faceplate at their flank. It was enough to turn Taylor's attention.

Tsengal, he thought. He would not say it aloud through risk of giving away his identity.

Taylor lifted his Assegai and pointed it at Demiran.

"This is between us now, and you cannot win. You cannot win because the human race won't be defeated!"

Demiran lifted his glaive and rushed at Taylor with a loud roar. Taylor spun aside from the first strike, and narrowly missing the second as Demiran used his trademark double strike, utilising the weight of the massive glaive to pendulum the long blade around. Its thrust then smashed into his shield, and the energy threw him off his feet and into a line of Mechs. Demiran rushed at him with a heavy strike, but Tsengal grabbed Taylor and threw him out of the way.

Gallo, who had been watching the fight, thought Tsengal to be attacking the Colonel and lifted his rifle, firing two shots into his chest to save Taylor.

"No!" yelled Taylor from the ground.

Demiran smiled.

"Another one of your friends? Shame."

Taylor got to his feet and kept his distance. He opened up the gap between his Assegai and shield just enough to invite a thrust, which Demiran fell for. He lunged quickly and powerfully forward. Instead of parrying, Taylor stepped aside a few centimetres and released his shield. The glaive passed between his left arm and body, and in one quick action Taylor wrapped his arm around the shaft, locking it against his body.

Demiran tried to tug the blade, but it was too late. Taylor threw his Assegai. It embedded in the creature's chest and forced him to release his grip. Taylor quickly grasped the shaft with his other hand also and spun it around and up over his head.

"This is for Chandra!" he cried, as he brought the blade down with all his strength. Demiran lifted his arm in defence, but the massive blade cut straight through and into his skull. Taylor released his grip, and the alien Lord fell flat to the ground with the glaive firmly embedded. All watching were utterly silent and could not think of a response. Taylor quickly remembered Tsengal and rushed to his body. He spun over his friend who was wearing a full Mech suit.

"Tsengal! Tsengal!"

The alien opened its eyes for a second and spat blood.

"He's alive! Get some help over here!" he shouted to his friends. The Mechs around him watched in utter shock as he held Tsengal like one of his own. Tsengal tried to speak but passed out.

"Get some God damn medical attention here!"

Jafar staggered over to see his comrade lying in Taylor's arms.

"He's alive?"

"Barely."

Taylor realised that it was still silent and looked up to the faceless Mechs. They were gazing at the scene. It was an odd sensation, but he knew he must address them. They could see two of their own with Taylor, and that alone was clearly confusing them.

"Demiran is dead. Your reason for being here is over. You don't have to keep fighting this war! Lay down your weapons, and you will not be harmed!"

It was obviously an alien concept to them. Many looked to Jafar for answers. He was the only one of their own race standing at Taylor's side. He nodded in agreement and added his own comments. Though he spoke in English, so both sides could understand.

"The war is over! Don't die for Demiran. He is no longer your master!"

With that comment, the first few Mechs began to drop their weapons in front of Taylor and Demiran's body. Several raised their faceplates, revealing themselves to the humans.

"Spread word through your army. This is over!" Taylor shouted.

The gunfire in the distance began to die down as the message was spread.

"This is Taylor to HQ. Demiran's army is laying down arms."

Phillips could not believe what he was hearing, but he too had watched the whole seen from the camera feeds. He looked along the line of screens to see battle had all but stopped. Many of the Mechs simply lay down their weapons and retreated back towards the K'til. Others just froze where they stood.

Medics began to pour onto the scene, and Jafar was quick to strip Tsengal's armour and carry him to one of the copters. The medics appeared utterly shocked at the sight. Few had ever seen the enemy alive, let alone had to treat one. Taylor moved to Tsengal's side, as he was loaded aboard the medical copter. He regained consciousness for just a few seconds, which gave them hope. He uttered just a few words.

"Red 1, hundreds of thousands of, of, pe..."

He faded out once again.

"Tsengal!"

There was nothing more Taylor would get from their alien friend.

"Go with him," he said to Jafar.

"Thank you."

Taylor stepped aside to let them lift off. Jones hobbled up to his position.

"What did he say?"

"God only knows. We can only hope he makes it."

"You really did it. It worked."

"No, we did it."

Gallo rushed to the Colonel, weeping.

"I am so sorry, Colonel. I thought, I thought."

"Save it, you couldn't have known. Tsengal is a tough one. He'll pull through."

Tsengal had not been able to deliver Chandra's message. Taylor could see whatever he had to say was important, and that bothered him, but for now he turned to the scene of carnage before them.

"We paid a heavy price here, Yorath, Monty, Blinker, all dead. I saw dozens of others drop but not sure who. Silva's in a bad way too, Mitch."

"Eli? Where is she?"

He turned, looking across the battlefield where they had made their charge. He couldn't believe she wouldn't have been there for the final fight. She staggered towards with him, using her rifle as a crutch. He rushed to her, grabbing her so tight thatshe squirmed in pain.

"God you scared me, Mitch."

"Demiran is dead, and most of the Mechs have surrendered or laid down arms."

She could barely believe it but sighed in relief.

"What do we do now?"

"What we fought all this time to do, live. Earth is ours."

Tsengal's words still preyed on Taylor's mind, but for now he knew they had entered a new age of peace. He was going to enjoy it while it lasted.